TIMBER WOLF

ALSO BY MURPHY LAWLESS

VIRTUE SHIFTERS

Timber Wolf * Librarian Bear * Sealed With A Kiss * Hold My Bear * A Christmas Like No Otter * Wear Wolf * A Very Meowy Christmas * Somebunny to Love * Buck the Halls * Koalafied For Love

GLADIATOR SHIFTERS

Gladiator Bear * Gladiator Cheetah * Gladiator Hawk * Gladiator Wolf * Gladiator Tiger

RENAISSANCE SHIFTERS

OctoBEARfest * Partridge in a Bear Tree * Renaissance Bear

SHAMROCK SAFARI SHIFTERS

Lion on Loan * Peacock on Parade * Gorilla in the Groove

WRITING AS C.E. MURPHY

THE WALKER PAPERS

Urban Shaman * Banshee Cries * Thunderbird Falls * Coyote Dreams * Cauldron Borne * Demon Hunts * Spirit Dances * Raven Calls * No Dominion * Mountain Echoes * Shaman Rises

THE OLD RACES UNIVERSE

Heart of Stone * House of Cards * Hands of Flame * Baba Yaga's Daughter * Year of Miracles * Kiss of Angels

MKP

TIMBER WOLF
ISBN-13 (print): 978-1-83557-044-9

Cover Art: Indigo Chick Designs

TIMBER WOLF

VIRTUE SHIFTERS

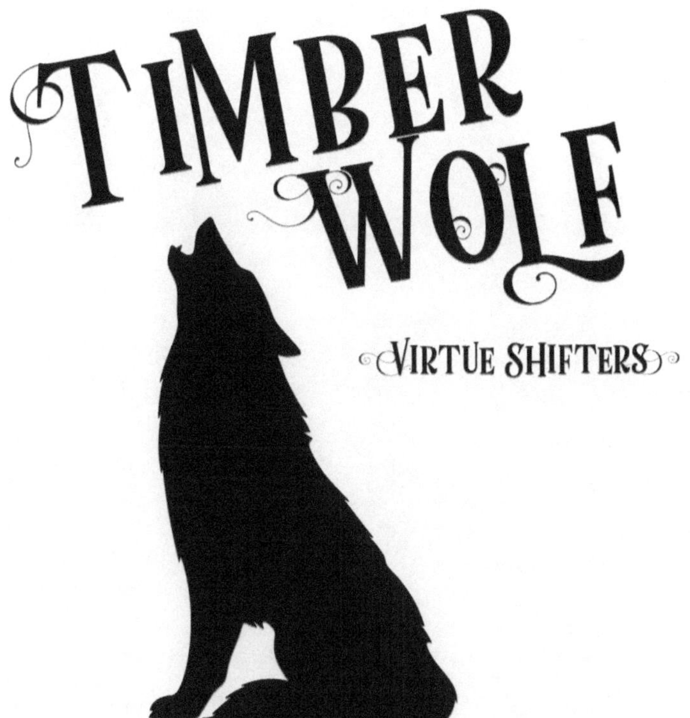

MURPHY LAWLESS WRITING AS
ZOE CHANT

CHAPTER 1

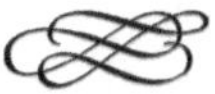

Renovating a farmhouse and living off the land wasn't nearly as romantic as Mabs Brannigan had thought it would be.

She'd inherited the house from a great-aunt she hadn't even known existed. It dated from the early 19th century—the house did, not the aunt, although apparently she'd been pretty old, too—and it looked like Aunt Doris had only lived in two rooms of the rambling old house for...a long time now. And neither of those rooms, it turned out, was a bathroom. Mabs had used an outhouse more in the past four months than she had in her entire life, including that one unfortunate summer camp when she was thirteen.

Aunt Doris had apparently kept the place running on hope and a smidgen of rent from a couple of acres where a neighbor kept her horses. But that wasn't enough to renovate on, and Mabs wouldn't have jumped at the chance for a falling-down farmhouse in upstate New York if she'd been flush with money. Until the beginning of the summer, when she and her son had moved to the farmhouse, she'd been waitressing in the city.

Now she was waitressing in Virtue, the small town a few miles away from the house, which was—honestly, it was better. The people were nice, and she'd made enough friends already that usually someone was willing to mind four-year-old Noah while Mabs was at work. It helped, of course, that he was mostly an outrageously charming kid, which definitely wasn't just her biased-mommy opinion on the matter.

One of those friends—Sarah Ekstrom, who effectively ran a daycare out of the local library—was on her way over to the house right now to watch Noah for a while so Mabs could get some renovation work done without a small child's 'help'.

Standing alone in the kitchen, Mabs pushed down a stab of panic and tears. Think about the good parts, she told herself. There was so much good about the old house. If she could just get it renovated....

Which she never would now, because the contractor had just skipped town with the last of her money.

She should have known better than to pay him in cash. She should have known...she didn't even know *what* she should have known. Mabs clutched her phone, trying not to think about the call from the hardware store, asking when she was going to pay them for the new copper fittings for the sink. A wave of dizziness had come over her as she'd whispered, "But I sent Chad over on Tuesday with the payment."

The store owner's voice had gone a terrible combination of sympathetic and determined as she'd told her Chad had never shown up. Mabs whispered a promise to pay her soon, then called around to the kitchen store, the cabinet-makers, the electrician and the plumber.

Nobody had seen her contractor since Monday, when they'd given him final quotes. Quotes that he'd brought back to Mabs, who had handed over the cash, thanked him for doing so much for her, and...

...and never seen him again. It was Saturday now, and nobody in town had seen Chad since Monday night. His apartment was cleared out, his car was gone, and Mabs...

Mabs was screwed, and not in the good way.

It was gonna be okay. It *had* to be okay. She and Noah didn't have anywhere else to go. She would figure it out, because she had to. Right now it was only mid-afternoon—she'd worked an early shift at the restaurant—so she could get a lot done before evening overtook her. Even if she was winging it. YouTube and do-it-yourself books could carry her a long way, but enthusiasm and tutorials didn't make up for a total lack of experience.

Panic surged through her again and she forced it down a second time, swallowing against the tightness in her throat.

"MAMA!" Noah came pounding down the stairs like a herd of elephants, threw the kitchen door open, and flung himself at her with the strength of a small tornado. Mabs caught him, staggered, and despite everything, laughed as he seized her face in both hands so he could look at her intently from five inches away. "Mama I'm *hungry* can I have a *cheese sandwich* and—" his blue-eyed expression went cunning— "*pickles?*"

Mabs squinted at him, trying not to smile. "I thought you didn't like cheese."

His expression went shiftier, gaze sliding back and forth as if searching the kitchen for an explanation that would satisfy his suspicious mother. "I might *now*."

"Or you might just want a bunch of pickles."

Noah's mouth and eyes both went perfectly round. "Mama! What a good idea!"

Mabs burst out laughing and put him down on the rough-hewn plank floor that had been worn smooth by time. "I'm a genius, aren't I?"

"Soooooper-genius!" Noah put his arms out and 'flew' with the drawn-out word, unconcerned with his safety as he careened around the kitchen. Mabs made a series of cut-off warning sounds as he ran, never quite actually damaging either himself or anything in the old kitchen.

They'd been in the house four months and Mabs hadn't quite gotten over the kitchen yet. It was amazing. Antiquated, maybe, but amazing. It—and most of the house—was still loaded with original features, if only she could fix everything *around* them. Aunt Doris had installed an Aga cooker in the 1940s, which made it not exactly original-to-the-house, but certainly antique. It still worked like a charm, even if Mabs had needed a crash course in using it, and it heated up both the whole kitchen and the bedroom above it, which would be useful, come winter, if she couldn't get the rest of the place fixed.

The fridge—also from the 40s—probably used more power than half of Virtue, but it was genuinely gorgeous in an obviously authentically retro way. Mabs pulled its door open, narrowly missing Noah, who continued bouncing around like a rubber ball, and got out a giant jar of cucumber chips. Noah skidded to a halt, complex disappointment dashing across his small face. "Don't we have any of the long ones?"

"Nope. I don't like dill pickles."

"*I* would eat them!" The degree of urgency placed in those four words could have powered the fridge for a week.

"Yeah, but what would I eat?"

Noah, disdainful as only a child could be, said, "Cheese sandwiches."

Mabs laughed. "But I only like them with pickles!"

Her son's eyebrows drew down as he considered this conundrum. Mabs, fishing pickles into a bowl with a fork, pointed at the kitchen door with her chin. "Close that, why don't you, so the heat stays in?"

Noah bounced over, closing the door with authority and shutting the rest of the house away. There were four rooms downstairs: the kitchen and a dining room behind it, and, across the hall, a large living room that the door stuck on, which didn't matter because the roof also leaked, as did the windows, and...yeah. There was a lot to do there.

Behind the parlor, across from the dining room, was what she'd learned had probably been a birthing room—basically a downstairs bedroom that a new mother, the elderly, or the infirm could use. She'd barely been in it; there was too much to do just to make a few rooms really livable, never mind trying to spruce up extra spaces.

Another kitchen door led out to what she guessed had been a buttery, once upon a time. It still had the butter churn, and Mabs had dreams of doing something with it, someday.

Someday.

Behind that was a whole other extension to the house that barely qualified as more than a ruin. All that functioned in it was a small, unpleasant toilet area that they used at night, but the outhouse was preferable during daylight hours. Mabs didn't let herself think about that side of the house at all, or the attic over the parlor side of the house, which she hadn't even ventured into, yet.

But if she opened both the kitchen doors and the parlor door she could see the whole length of the front of the house with its original wooden floors, and the narrow stairway leading up to five bedrooms, with the attic above three of them. It was a genuinely amazing old place. All she needed to do was get it suitable to really live in, and then she and Noah would be...safe.

She shook herself as she got the pickles. They hadn't been *unsafe*. It was just that Noah's father...

Mabs made a sound under her breath. Noah's dad wasn't interested in being a dad. He just didn't want Mabs to move on, or have a life, or be certain of any choices she made, ever, unless he approved of them.

He gaslit you, she reminded herself firmly. There was nothing wrong with the decisions she made. Noah's father had just...taken her confidence away.

Her cell phone rang as she put Noah's pickles on his plate. She sat him, and them, at the long wooden table that sat beneath one of the house's many windows, and answered with a breathless, "Yeah?"

"Mabs, hi, this is Sarah, look, a friend I haven't seen in a while stopped by just before I left the house. He's into old houses and I was wondering if it'd be okay if he came with me? I bet he can tell you things you never knew you never knew about Doris's place."

Mabs bared her teeth in what she pretended was a smile. "Maybe he can tell me how to fix the whole place up on a budget of zero dollars and no cents. Or maybe that's no *sense*...."

"Mama?" Noah looked up from his pickles, innocent gaze concerned. "Are you sad, Mama? Are you mad? You can use your words and tell me," he said encouragingly.

Mabs blurted a laugh and went over to kiss the top of his curly head. "I'm okay, baby. Thank you. I love you."

"I love you too." Noah offered her a pickle, as proof. She accepted it, because what kind of hard-hearted monster wouldn't?

"Thank you, honey."

"You're welcome," both Noah and Sarah, in Mabs's ear, said. She laughed again, and Sarah said, "We'll be there soon. It's gonna be okay, Mabs."

"Yeah." Mabs's voice was hoarse, but she nodded. "I'm sure it will be."

"Is that Auntie Sarah?" Noah asked hopefully. "Is she coming over to play with me?"

Mabs said, "She *is*," as she hung up. "She's bringing a friend, too, but he wants to look at the house, not play with kids."

Noah's expression said what he thought of that, but, reasonably content with his pickles, he didn't complain. Mabs got a glass of water and stood in front of the sink, trying to get the tap to stop leaking and trying to keep her eyes from *starting* to leak. Her phone rang and she startled badly enough to fumble it, and had to take it from the bottom of the wet sink to answer the unknown number with a shaky, "Hello?"

"Hi, my name is Preston Cole with Cole Realty. May I speak to Mary Anne Brannigan, please?"

"This is she."

"Great, hi, Ms. Brannigan. Look, I don't want to waste your time, so let me get straight to the point. I'm—"

"Representing the developer who wants to buy the farm?" Mabs sounded weary to her own ears. There had been a lot of paperwork with the inheritance of the farmhouse, and she'd gone through it all slowly, sometimes struggling to understand what it meant. One part that hadn't been hard, though, was the cash offer from some development company who wanted to build a mall or something where her house was.

Mabs had thrown it away. Aunt Doris's house was *hers* now, and she was determined to keep it. Businessmen in expensive suits had come sniffing around a couple of times already and she'd run them off, but Preston Cole, and Cole Realty, were local. She guessed they were trying the soft touch now.

"I was Doris Brannigan's realtor," Preston said with what sounded like genuine sympathy. "She was prepared to sell, before she died. I was hoping you and I could pick up where she and I left off."

"Four months later?"

"Actually, it's been almost a year," Preston said. "It took the estate executors a while to find you, Ms. Brannigan. I've been out of town, and didn't know you'd moved in. I wish I'd caught you before you did."

"Well, thank you for calling, but I'm not interested in selling."

"It's a half-million dollar deal, Ms. Brannigan."

Mabs's knees buckled, but she caught herself on the counter. Butcher-block counter, oiled and sanded through the generations. You literally couldn't buy that kind of quality.

But she had $113.44 in her bank account, and half a million dollars would solve all her problems, maybe forever. Eyes closed, heart pounding, Mabs whispered, "I'm not interested in selling, Mr. Cole," and didn't even believe herself.

"I'll call again soon," Preston said in a gentle voice.

He'd barely hung up when Sarah knocked on the door, shouted, "We're here!" and walked in with the most gorgeous man Mabs had ever seen.

CHAPTER 2

Jake Rowly remembered the old Brannigan place from when he was a kid. Doris Brannigan had been a kind old woman even then, although in retrospect, he supposed she hadn't been all *that* old. Maybe in her sixties, which didn't seem so old now, from the thick side of forty himself.

Regardless, everybody in Virtue called it *the old Brannigan place*, because it had been around for a couple centuries, regardless of how old its current occupant was. And he'd hung around the place a bit, especially in the fall when the apples were ripening—

So we could filch them, his wolf said with a note of age-old satisfaction.

Jake winced. *We shouldn't have done that.*

Why not? **She** *wasn't eating them.*

Yeah, but we should have at least asked. It's not polite to just go around stealing peoples' food.

Cubs do it all the time, his wolf replied airily.

And at the time, Jake supposed, he'd been close enough to a cub to count. Certainly too young to recognize the quality of the old farmhouse's build, anyway.

But now, peering at it as they approached in Sarah Ekstrom's boxy old red truck, he could appreciate its bones, even if the poor old house was falling down around itself. The trees he remembered from childhood had mostly succumbed to Dutch Elm disease, leaving only one or two to keep the summer sun from broiling the front rooms of the house, and the glimpse he got of the back extension said its roof had pretty well given up the ghost.

There were gaps around windows, and a swaybacked roof ridge on the main body of the house. Some inexpert repairs had been made to the wide front door, which had been painted a cheery bright yellow since he'd last seen it. He sat back against the hard springs of the truck seat and glanced at Sarah. "You're trying to set me up."

Sarah, a striking woman who drove like she was in a road rally race, slid a falsely innocent smile at him. "Would I do that?"

"Yeah."

"Well, you're a carpenter, Jake, and it's a house that needs carpenting. And Mabs is nice."

Doris Brannigan had been ninety if she'd been a day, when she'd died. Presumably any heirs of hers would be in their mature years as well, and God knew the house needed more work than an old lady could manage. He'd heard the new Ms. Brannigan had a son, but judging from the house's condition, he wasn't the handy type.

"Nice is fine, but I hope she's *rich,* " Jake said aloud. "The cost of giving this place the TLC it needs is going to be catastrophic."

"Yeah, well, you know, all of us rich Virtue-ese, sneaking around hiding our wealth in mattresses instead of the bank." Sarah pulled the truck up outside the farmhouse gates and swung out of the vehicle to march up to the door, knock, shout, "We're here!" and walk in without waiting for an answer.

Jake, following her, took in the broad, short hall with its narrow staircase, the impression of an old, old chimney in the wall across from the stairs, and built a picture of the kitchen in his mind before he even stepped through the second door that Sarah pushed open.

One step through, though, and he forgot everything he'd ever known about architecture, or even carpentry, because Mary Anne Brannigan wasn't sixty and fragile, not one little bit.

She was in her thirties and small, with the kind of round softness that often hid a lot of strength. She wore long hair loose and gently purple around a heart-shaped face, a black t-shirt with some kind of crazily-horned golden helmet and the words *Say My Name* printed on it. Jake, with a rush of heat, thought of a *number* of circumstances he'd like to say her name in. Her jeans hugged her waist and hips and thighs in the most attractive way possible before flaring at the calf until they looked like the bottom of a skirt. He could see half a tattoo under one shirt sleeve, and an ankh necklace peeking out of her neckline.

She was, in other words, *exactly* Jake's type, and Sarah Ekstrom knew it.

Sarah *knows it?* his wolf asked incredulously. *You can't tell when fate throws your* **mate** *at you?*

'Exactly my type' is not the same as 'fated mate', Jake replied ruefully, and besides—

And besides, there was a four-year-old bellowing, "Auntie Saaaaaaraaaaaaah!" and throwing himself away from the kitchen table to tackle Sarah's hips. Even if Jake was hoping to find the woman fate wanted him to be with—and he wasn't, not after last time—no shifter in his right mind would walk up to a lady with a child and say *hey, fate says it's you and me, babe. How 'bout it?*

Or a lady without a child, for that matter. Not unless he wanted to get punched, anyway.

But I'm riiiiiiiiiiight. The wolf's voice sounded like a smug howl rising from Jake's soul. His gaze left the little boy and returned to Mary Anne Brannigan, whose soft smile for her kid said she was obviously pleased by his delight.

Jake dearly wanted that same soft smile to be directed at *him.* Given how gun-shy he was about love right then, he was afraid the wolf was right. But even if it was—

Smugly: *I am.*

Even if you are, Jake thought strongly, as if he could argue half of who he was into submission, *even if you are, I'm not rushing into anything. Not with a kid in the picture. Besides...I need some time, too.*

A bit of sympathy melted through him and the wolf stopped being pushy, settling down as Sarah staggered back a couple steps, laughing, and scooped the little boy up. "Hey, munchkin. Ready to explore the deep dark woods while your mom gets some work done around here?"

The kid's eyes sparkled and he lowered his voice conspiratorially. "I found a *wolf den* in the forest."

Sarah, amused, said, "Really? Wolf, huh? Not gruffalo?" as Jake stiffened with caution. The kid obviously couldn't *know* Jake was a wolf shifter, but that was an unusual thing to hear five seconds after meeting somebody.

His wolf gave a lazy shake, as if casting off a cub's practice attack. *It might be,* it said, *if we hadn't **left a den** in the orchard when we were young.*

A flash of memory hit Jake: the scent of loamy earth, the warmth of sunshine filtering through the trees, the rustle of wind and the thump of falling apples, all experienced from within a well-dug, cozy den. He hadn't thought of that childhood hideaway in years. Decades, even. He would never have imagined it still existed, much less in good enough condition for an intrepid four-year-old explorer to discover. He looked at the kid—Noah—with a degree of admiration that the child utterly failed to notice.

"Gruffalos aren't *real,*" Noah said with obvious derision.

"Noah, be polite," said his mother.

The little boy looked guilty and sparkled his eyes at

Sarah. "I'm sorry for being rude. I shouldn't do that because it hurts people's feelings. I won't do it again."

Sarah kissed his hair. "All is forgiven. Wolves may be real and gruffalos pretend, but a gruffalo is about as likely around here as a wolf. I don't think anybody's seen one in these parts in the last fifty years. Sorry, I didn't make introductions. Mabs, this is Jake Rowly. Jake, this is Mary Anne and Noah Brannigan, they inherited the place and Mabs is working on renovating."

"A pleasure." Jake's voice came out two octaves deeper than he meant it to as he offered his hand to Mary Anne. A lovely flush climbed her cheeks as she put her hand in his. She had a strong grip, like she was confident in herself.

"Nice to meet you, Mr. Rowly."

Jake rolled his eyes and a broad grin flashed across Mary Anne's face. "Let me guess: Mr. Rowly is your father?"

"Well, to me, he was 'sir', but...yeah. Please, call me Jake."

"Mary Anne, but please call me Mabs," she said, "and this is Noah. Which Sarah already said, so...I guess we've got that pretty thoroughly covered. Hey, um, Noah, could you go upstairs and get that thing you wanted to show Sarah?"

The child's eyebrows drew down and he looked at his mother in confusion for a few seconds before his expression cleared. He yelled, "Yeah!" and ran from the room with the energy and noise of a steam engine.

Sarah, after watching him go, said, "What did he want to show me?" in a mystified tone.

"I have no idea. I just figured there was probably something, and I needed to get him out of the room." Mabs cast Jake a brief, pained glance, as if to apologize for something in advance, and said, "Did you hear about Chad?"

A misplaced sense of protective outrage rose in Jake's chest. He'd met this woman seventy seconds ago. He had no idea who Chad was. He shouldn't feel the urge to go hunt him down and—

A vivid image of hamstringing prey leaped to his mind, his wolf's presence a low growl at the back of his mind. Jake shook his head, trying to dislodge the general sense of approval he felt at the idea.

As he wrestled with those unexpected impulses, Sarah's expression collapsed into sympathy. "I did. It's all over town. I'm so sorry, Mabs. It sucks."

Mabs sagged against the kitchen chair her son had vacated. "I don't know. I just don't know. He was my contractor," she explained to Jake. "He was supposed to..." She made a helpless gesture at the house. "He took off with my money instead."

"Aw, hell. I'm sorry to hear it." He was more than sorry. He wanted to huff and puff and...blow Chad down, he guessed. The old fairy tale didn't really scan very well in these circumstances.

She gave him a terrible mess of a smile. She wasn't quite crying, but Jake wanted to wipe away her tears anyway, gather her into his arms, and promise it would all be okay.

*You **should**,* his wolf said in tones that implied he was an idiot.

And maybe Jake was, but even if the wolf was right, the last thing he was looking for was romance. Not after the way things had gone last time. *Last time* was why Jake was back in Virtue, a town he'd left after graduating high school, at all. He wrenched his mind away from the thought, and his wolf grumbled.

Before he could take any irrevocably stupid actions, though, a tremendous rattling sounded on the stairs. A heartbeat later, Noah burst back through the door with ten feet worth of plastic car tracks bouncing along behind him. "Lookit this, Auntie Sarah! Watch, the cars go by themselves!" He threw the whole track on the floor, stared around, shouted, "I forgot the cars!" and went tearing back out the door.

For a few seconds all three adults just looked at where he'd been, as if the whirlwind that was Noah would simply reappear, or start up again, without warning. Jake finally said, "Wow," and Mabs made another pained face, this one much fonder than the first.

"Welcome to the life of single motherhood. It's part of why I need a contractor." She pinched her forehead, then slid her hand back through the dark lilac tones of her hair. It fell back around her face in straight lines as she sighed. "I just really can't get any traction on renovations when I'm chasing him around, even if I had the skills, which, honestly, I don't."

Jake opened his mouth to offer sympathies, and instead heard himself say, "But I do."

CHAPTER 3

Tall, broad-shouldered, ruggedly handsome men did not just wander into Mabs's life and offer to do home reconstruction for her. They just *didn't*. That was the only thing preventing Mabs from shrieking, "Yes, oh my God, would you please?!" in Jake Rowly's face.

Or in his breastbone, if she was to be brutally honest about it. Mabs knew she had many excellent features, but an excess of height wasn't one of them. Jake Rowly stood a splendid eight inches taller than she did, and had the strong build of a man who'd been doing hard work all his life. He'd obviously gone grey early, because he couldn't be more than a handful of years older than she was, but he had hardly any brown left in its short length.

Not that her own hair wasn't doctored a bit by the fine products of the hair and beauty industry, but Mabs wasn't really trying to hide her handful of grey hairs with the purple she'd favored for years.

Anyway, the grey suited Rowly's summer-brown skin and the electric blue of his eyes, and the piercing in his left ear, and the dark red of his well-fitted button-down shirt, which he'd rolled the long sleeves up on to expose his strong forearms, good *God*, his forearms, and...Mabs wet her lips and tried to remember what they'd been talking about. Sarah had said she was bringing a friend, not that she was bringing a fabulously attractive single man.

Or at least, Mabs hoped he was single. Not that she needed the complication of a romance with the house and Noah and her job and everything, but... *damn*. On general principle she needed Jake Rowly to be single, just so there was some hope left in the world.

She could not remember the last time she'd laid eyes on a man so attractive that she'd forgotten what they were talking about. With effort she wrenched her brain back to the topic at hand, which was...Jake Rowly casually saying *he* had the skills to fix up her house.

Hoping she hadn't been silently gaping like a fish for too long, Mabs released a shaky laugh and shook her head. "That'd be amazing, but I couldn't pay you. I *can't* pay you. I'm not sure how I'm going to pay for groceries, right now."

The kitchen door burst open again and Noah reappeared, his arms full of battery-operated toy cars. Rattling noises behind him on the stairs and in the hallway suggested that he had been even more toy-laden when he left his bedroom, but had lost a fair number of vehicles on the way. "Now I can show you, Auntie Sarah!"

"Tell you what," Sarah said smoothly, "why don't you bring those out to the porch and start setting up, and I'll be out before you can blink twice."

Noah squeezed his big blue eyes open and shut a couple of times, caroled, "Nuh-uh!", and rushed outdoors to drop the cars with another clatter. He returned at full speed, got the car tracks, and exited again with them banging behind him like a plastic dragon's tail. The door slamming shut behind him was almost anti-climactic.

Silence enveloped the adults again, as if respect had to be paid to the amount of sheer energy they'd just seen expended. Mabs didn't exactly notice it so much when there weren't other people around, but Noah had a real knack for dominating the space he was in.

Sarah, though, picked up the thread of conversation as if it hadn't been interrupted, thanks to a lot of prac-tice at the library-daycare. "The thing is, though, Mabs, Jake's just back in town and he doesn't have anywhere to stay, so I was thinking, like, your barn's pretty solid, right? You could snug up a corner of that and Jake could stay there and work on the house."

"He can't stay in my *barn*. It's a *barn*! You can't stay in my *barn*!" Mabs's gaze flickered between Sarah and Jake, finally landing accusingly on Sarah. "Have you been *planning* this?!"

"I don't see how I could have been," Sarah said in the cheerful tone of someone who had been planning this. "I only found out about Chad this morning and then Jake only dropped by the library about half an hour ago to say he was back in town. Who has time to plan?"

"You!" Both Mabs and Jake spoke, then exchanged little grins that made Mabs want to giggle like a schoolgirl. Jake Rowly had a sly, charming grin that could seduce a woman at five paces. Or maybe seven, since that's about how far away from she was.

"I have not been planning anything," Sarah said loftily. "I do, however, see an opportunity when it presents itself. You two talk it out. I have a date with a car race." She exited with less fanfare than Noah had, leaving Mabs and Jake and a whole lot of uncomfortable space between them.

Jake broke it. "I had no idea she was going to do that. Sorry."

"No, not at all. I didn't either, obviously. And it's not that you can't stay in my barn, it's just—" Mabs gestured broadly, as if it would explain everything she meant. "It's just, who goes around inviting people to stay in *barns*?"

"Apparently Sarah," Jake said dryly. They both laughed, and suddenly the tension evaporated, leaving Mabs smiling easily at...at the strange man in her house. Maybe she shouldn't dwell on that.

"Sarah's always been a fixer-upper," Jake added. "Even in high school she was always trying to make things work better. She ran our student body single-handedly. I guess I kind of thought she'd be mayor of Virtue by now."

"I don't think she has time, with running the library and the not-officially-a-daycare and helping out with Meals-On-Wheels and overseeing the allotment gardens and..." Mabs trailed off. "I see what you mean."

She fell silent a moment, then cleared her throat. "What you said...would you *want* to?"

"What, fix up this place?" Jake's blue gaze rose to the kitchen ceiling, which Mabs bet he could touch easily. She needed a chair to get to the top shelf of the dang cupboards, and they were only two shelves high. "Yeah," Jake said with a touch of longing that Mabs frankly wished was directed at her. "I could do wonders with this old house. Somebody should, anyway. Do you know anything about its construction?"

His gaze returned to Mabs with the power of a static shock. Her breath caught and she straightened a little, like electricity really had run through her. "Um. No? Not really? I know it's from about the mid-1800s, but that's about it?"

Jake shook his head and actually offered her his hand, like they'd known each other forever. What was even stranger was that she took it like it was natural. His grip was comfortable, his hand strong and calloused from work. Mabs had never liked super soft hands anyway. There were so many places on her body where the roughness of a callous could add a little extra... *hrrr.*

God, what was she thinking? Well obviously she knew exactly what she was thinking, but it was, as she liked to tell Noah about some of his more outlandish ideas, *wildly inappropriate.*

Jake smiled and drew her out of her own house, leading her past Noah and Sarah on the porch, and down the steps. Mabs had to look at her feet to make sure they were still on the ground, because somehow, holding Jake Rowly's work-strong hand made her feel like she was floating.

When they got out to the yard, he turned her to face the house, and then, as if he'd suddenly realized what he was doing, let go of her hand. "Sorry, that was..."

"No, it's fine, I could have kicked you instead of taking your hand." It took all of Mabs's attention to not put a hand over her face. She sounded like an eight year old. "What did you want to show me?"

His smile appeared again, no longer sly, but genuine and sweet as he lifted his hands toward the house and began pointing. "So from the door over to the left, basically your kitchen, the room behind it, and the rooms above? That was probably the original house. They called it a double-cell, double-pile."

"Catchy," Mabs muttered, and Jake grinned.

"Isn't it, though? So back then, where your hallway is, that was the front."

Mabs said, "But this is the front," and winced. Now she sounded like an idiot. She was a waitress, for heaven's sake. She was *good* at talking to people, even about things she didn't care about, and she *did* care about the house.

But Jake was still grinning like she wasn't an idiot, so maybe it was okay. "Right, this is the front now. But when it started, back probably around 1790—you could look it up in the local records—it was the side."

"Oh. Wow. I never thought of looking it up in the records. I've never lived anywhere old enough to have local records, I don't think."

"Most of us haven't, but this place, everybody knows it."

"'The Old Brannigan Place,' yeah. People in Virtue are always excited to hear there's someone living here again." Mabs smiled at the truth of that. It was one of the reasons she simply didn't want to give the place up. "Okay, so this was the side?"

"Right, and you know how the roof is a different height over the kitchen side of the house?" At Mabs's nod, Jake went on. "That's because *this* part of the house, from about here over..." He jogged over to the farthest wall to the right of the kitchen—which was quite a ways to the right, maybe 25 feet—and spread his arms like he'd pick up a piece of the house. His jeans fit *really* well. Really, really, *really* well. Like... *really* well.

Mabs yanked her attention away from Jake's backside, caught Sarah's gaze, and tried not to blush as Sarah winked before going back to playing with Noah. Mabs grimaced, but looked back at Jake, who was talking over his shoulder to her.

"This was probably a second house, built freestanding but with the intention to expand *toward* the original house. So they both faced each other, see?" He sounded so excited that Mabs started to smile. "Then as the Brannigan income and family size grew, they expanded the newer house toward the older one until it became one."

Mabs blinked back and forth at the whole front of the house, trying to wrap her brain around it. "So *all* of this used to be the sides of the house...es? Until they connected it? I wondered why the roof was higher over the right side of the house, but...I had no idea!"

"Yep, these were the sides, but once the buildings were connected, it became the front, and they put the porch on. And then sometime later they added the buttery on the other side of the kitchen, and probably even later than *that* they rearranged everything inside that wasn't a load-bearing wall." He suddenly looked abashed and came back from gesturing at the house's walls. "Sorry if I went on about it. It's an exciting bit of old architecture."

"No, it's amazing." Mabs came forward to stand beside him, looking up at the different heights of the roofs. The attic was over the newer part, the one Jake had described as the second original house. "So we've really been living in the very oldest part of the house. I couldn't tell."

"Yeah, the whole idea of the exterior renovations, back in the day, was to make it look like it had always been a single unit. That's where we get these long slats running horizontally across the front. They moved all the doors around, put in new windows, made it symmetrical, and boarded it so it looked like it had been built this way on purpose."

"Life hack," Mabs said, almost under her breath, but Jacob Rowly grinned down at her.

"That's what I think of it as, too. Then there's an extension behind the buttery, right?"

"Yeah, so the whole house is a kind of wonky L-shape and you can't get from the parlor to the rooms behind the buttery without going on a half-mile walk.

And the butter extension is only single-story so the roofs are all over the place, like..." Mabs drew it in the air: two and a half stories for the parlor side of the house, two for the kitchen side, then one for the buttery and rooms behind it. "It's a mess."

"What do you want to do with it?" Jake turned his attention from the house to Mabs, regarding her with the same intensity he'd examined the walls with.

Heat started burning along her collarbones and crept upward to the line of her jaw. She knew the look was for her planned renovations, not her, but... *dang.* The impulse to look at her feet and mumble like a shy teenager was high. Very, very high.

Mabs swallowed instead, tried not to look too hard at Jake's lips—he had very nice lips—and said, "Well, Chad was supposed to get the kitchen up to some kind of modern specs, for one. Right now it's kind of the main heating source for the house, and the roof needs work, and there are just a lot of corners and spaces where I'm afraid Noah will fall through the floor or something, and—?"

Jake held up his hands. "A lot of that's not under my skill set, but the roof and floors are."

"What *is* your skill set?"

"I'm a carpenter." Jake folded his hands down again, smiling, and Mabs watched them go into his jeans pockets.

Good hands. Long fingers. Nice nails. She already knew they were strong, from holding one briefly. There were a lot of things long, strong hands could do....

Including, apparently, carpentry. Mabs yanked her gaze to the house, reminding herself that that was what they were talking about, even if she kept being...distracted...by Jake's gorgeousness and his calm presence. It was completely insane to even *consider* having a stranger move onto the land, even if he was going to live in the barn, which was also insane. But Jake Rowly felt *safe* in a way Mabs couldn't remember ever encountering before. Like he would take care of her, Noah, and the house, all without ever asking anything in return.

Without knowing she'd made the decision, she returned her gaze to Jake. "Want to check out your room in the barn?"

CHAPTER 4

*A*n explosion of pure joy shattered through Jake's chest. Mary Anne Brannigan was looking up at him with the sweetest, most hopeful expression imaginable, and he thought he could probably die happy right then and there.

Faaaaaa-aaaaaate, said his wolf in a sing-song howl.

Jake said, *oh, shut up,* without rancor and the wolf laughed, which was fine, because Jake was afraid he had a kind of idiotic smile anyway, so at least they were on the same page. "I'd love to see the barn," he said, "but tell you what. Sarah's getting us into this in the first place, so how about I crash on her couch over the weekend and come over here to work, and we can see if it really works out before committing to anything more serious?"

Mabs's green eyes widened and she stuck out a hand to shake. "Yeah, that's a deal, but you also have to write a book called *How to be a Better Boyfriend* or

something, because wow, that's like top-notch consid-
eration there."

The wolf said, *Boyfriend!* in smug delight. Jake
stuffed that down and shook both Mabs's hand and his
head. "I'm not sure about a book. I'm better with my
hands than words."

A blush started somewhere below Mabs's ankh
necklace and worked its way up. Jake wondered, with
great interest, whether it was working its way *down*,
too, and how far, and decided he'd better not ask. It
was enough that making a comment about being good
with his hands got a blush out of this exceptionally
perfect woman.

Even if he absolutely, definitely, 100% was not
interested in a relationship right now.

He was still holding Mabs's hand. He thought he
should probably let go, but he didn't really want to. She
had small hands, like the rest of her. Most of the rest of
her: the figure-hugging t-shirt, and the way those crazy
golden horns expanded across her chest, made it pretty
clear that *some* parts of her were proportionately
generous, and...

...and he really couldn't just kneel, bury his face in
her breasts, wrap his arms around her hips, and hold
on like he'd found a lifeline he hadn't even known he
was looking for.

Faaaaaa-aaaated maaaa-aaate, his wolf sang, and
anybody who could hear it would be able to tell that it
was teasing him. It was too bad for Jake that he was the
only one who *could* hear it. Or maybe it was good,

because that way nobody else knew he was being teased.

Finally, reluctantly, he released Mabs's hand, trying to think of something to say after *I'm good with my hands* that wouldn't sound hopelessly double-entendre-y.

To his huge relief, Sarah came to his rescue, calling, "Did I hear somebody taking my name in vain?" from the porch.

Mabs curled her hand against her chest like she was clinging to the memory of holding his hand, and turned toward Sarah. "Yeah, Jake's going to crash on your couch over the weekend."

"Oh, he is, is he?"

Noah piped, "Can *I* crash on your couch?" and slammed about five cars together demonstratively.

All three of the adults laughed. Sarah said, "Not that kind of crashing," to him, and nodded toward Jake. "All right, sounds good. Look, Mabs, I thought I might take Noah into town for dinner at the restaurant, if that's okay?"

Mabs cast Jake a quick look. "That'd be great? We could maybe try to get some work started?" At his nod, she smiled toward Sarah. "Yeah, that'd be great. His bedtime is 8, so have him back before then?"

"Oh my God, you expect me to be able to feed a ravenous four-year-old in only five hours? Whatever shall I do? C'mon, kiddo." Sarah scooped Noah under her arm like a sack of potatoes and carried him, shrieking with laughter, to give his mother a hug around the waist, and then to her truck. She stuck

Noah in the front seat, pulled a safety seat from the truck's bed, and got them both arranged in an appropriate manner while Jake looked on with admiration. He'd never gotten the hang of lacing the seat belts through the safety seats properly, but then, he hadn't had much opportunity to practice, either.

Maybe he would now, though.

His wolf sang, *You wiiiiiillll!*

Jake tried to hush it again, mumbling, *Even if I wanted to, and I don't know that I do, this isn't the time to even think about it.*

The wolf, exasperated, said, *Of course it is*, but subsided as Sarah called out to Jake.

"I'll be back to pick you up later, Jake. Behave, or I'll put you in this seat yourself." A moment later they drove off to the sound of Noah's gales of laughter. Apparently the idea of Jake in a child's safety seat was pretty funny.

To be fair, both he and Mabs were grinning about it, too. She said, "I wouldn't put it past her," and Jake lifted his hands as if in surrender.

"I wouldn't even try to fight her. She's a pistol."

His wolf conveyed horror in the way that only canine faces could, a mix of betrayal and shock filling the inside of Jake's head. *I would fight her!*

Jake chuckled silently and shot back an image of Sarah, as a teenager, breaking up a dog fight with a long stick and an overwhelming amount of bravery. *Don't bet you'd win.*

The wolf's ears flattened in dismay. *Oh yeah.*

"So you've known her a long time?" Mabs gestured

at the house, inviting him back in. They went into the kitchen, which still had the remnants of the house's original fireplace against the wall closest to the entry hall. Piecemeal counters of different lengths and heights, each a separate component that could be moved around. It felt, Jake thought with quiet astonishment, like home.

He hadn't felt that way about anywhere he'd lived in...longer than he cared to imagine. And he knew, whether his wolf put a voice to it or not, that it had less to do with the old house than the small, determined woman in it.

The wolf, satisfied that it didn't have to comment, gave one of those contented huffs that canines excelled in, and left Jake to his own devices. "Yeah, Sarah and I have been friends since we were about six, but I left Virtue after high school and hadn't really seen her since. My folks downsized and moved to Montana a couple years ago, which is why I don't have anywhere to stay. I'm over-explaining things, aren't I?"

Mabs smiled. "Saves me asking nosy questions. So. Here we have a kitchen." Her smile fell away as she looked up and down the length of the room. "Chad spent all summer working up plans, pricing things, and getting ready to work once we had all the material on hand, and then just took off with the money, so now I'm...screwed. I've insulated the floor—"

As soon as she said that, Jake crouched, examining one of the wider gaps between the venerable floorboards. Darkness looked back up at him, so he took his phone out, turning its flashlight on and shining it into the gap. A dull reflection shone back, and he looked up with a smile. "You've already got draft strips in? As well as insulation from below?"

Mabs gave him a weak smile in return. "Draft strips were one of the things I could do *with* Noah. His little fingers were great for stuffing them in there. And there's a cellar, so putting insulation between the joists wasn't too hard. I've got ambitions of putting up a barrier on the bottom side of the joists to add a little more insulation, but..." She spread her hands. "Money."

Jake's own bank account wasn't exactly overflowing, but he still bit back the offer to simply pay for it himself, knowing instinctively that Mabs wouldn't appreciate it. Instead he said, "Well, you've done a good job already. What about the walls?"

"I'm terrified of wrecking them," she confessed. "All this wood..." She gestured at the kitchen, which was lined by rich old planks top, side, and bottom. "I'd like to insulate the upstairs floors, too. We already did the draft strips up there, but if I could get insulation *between* the floors..."

"Well, that's where I'm your man."

*You **should** be her man.*

Wolves, Jake thought, were not particularly subtle creatures. Not that he could completely disagree with the wolf, but...this wasn't the time. It might be the place, though. He could all but feel Mabs's love for it, and knew he was half in love himself.

With the idea of restoring the old house, he told himself firmly. That was all he could afford, or want, to be in love with. "I have a lot of practice at taking old boards down without damaging them, and in most cases we only need to take a couple down anyway. Then we blow insulation in and board it up again, and *voila*." He snapped, and Mabs's hope shone through.

"Really? That's amazing. I thought we had to take them all down and I couldn't figure out how I was going to do that and still keep the historical society's permission to renova...no, they don't like calling it renovation. Re...habilitate..." She laughed, a deeper, richer sound than Jake had expected. "Reformat," she went on cheerfully. "Refurbish. Remodel. Restore! I have a terrible time remembering that word."

"You've talked to the historical society already?" Jake's admiration, already considerable, grew more. Or maybe that wasn't his admiration, but he'd just keep thinking of it that way, and hope his jeans didn't tell a different story. "Did you have any problems with them?"

"Honestly I think they were thrilled somebody wanted to fix the place up instead of rip it down. And I just want..." To Jake's surprise and a little to his dismay, her eyes filled with tears and her voice grew hoarse. "I just want it to be a place somebody loves. A safe home for Noah to grow up in."

His wolf whined, trying to push its way forward. Jake resisted, not ready to drop *I'm a shapeshifter* on Mabs just yet, but he empathized with the wolf's desire to shift and offer its furry shoulders to hug and cry on. Hardly anybody could keep crying when a wolf's long warm tongue was there to lick up the tears, but...yeah, that would be a little much right now.

Mabs pushed at her cheekbones with the heels of her hands, just below her eyes. "Sorry," she said, still hoarsely. "It's been kind of a day."

"I understand," he said as gently and warmly as he could. "Tell you what. It sounds like the kitchen is our priority? And then the bedrooms, to winterize the whole place, if nothing else?"

"Yeah." Mabs gave him a watery smile that was, at least, stronger than her last one. "I've spent an awful lot of the last few months just trying to clean up, if you want to know the truth. I don't think the old Ms. Brannigan was a hoarder, exactly. The house wasn't gross with old food or cat urine or anything, but it was...full. Like she didn't get out much for a long time, and didn't have any way to get rid of the not-gross stuff that built up. I've made about a thousand dumpster runs. Between that and work and Noah it hasn't left a lot of time for even trying to get the bigger stuff done around here. Even if I had the skills. Wow. Hi, I'm just going to dump all my feels on you. Sorry."

"I don't mind at all." Jake was surprised at how much he meant that, although his wolf wasn't. "Feel free to dump your feels any time. I'll keep them safe."

Mabs gave a startled, wet laugh. "Okay. Great. Thanks. But yes. Kitchen first, I think, then the two bedrooms above us, then...everything else."

"'Everything else' is probably too much to do at once, but..." Jake pointed his chin toward the boarded ceiling. "Why don't we get a couple of those panels down and see how much insulation we can blow in?

Same with the walls? And then tomorrow I'll rent a blower—?"

"I can't pay for that," Mabs blurted.

"Not now," he agreed. "But eventually you'll find a way, and in the meantime we can't insulate the place without a blower, so I'll rent one and you can really hate that while also recognizing its grim necessity."

Mabs stared at him, her jaw working as if she couldn't decide between a wry grin and a horrendous scowl. She landed, narrowly, on the side of the grin, although if a grin could scowl, hers did. "Yeah, that's...dammit. What, do I have pages, or something? Because you're reading me like a book."

Jake, after a long silence, said, "No, but I feel like that ought to have been my line, somehow...."

She finally laughed again, a real laugh. "It kind of sounded like it, didn't it? Okay, well, I think we can move everything but the Aga, if we need to. There's room in the buttery for most of the counters, I bet."

"Are you sure?" Jake glanced dubiously at the smaller room on the kitchen's far end, but Mabs cracked her knuckles and grinned.

"I'm a master at real-life Tetris. I can fit anything anywhere." She clamped her mouth shut and went crimson.

Jake couldn't help it. He laughed out loud. Mabs, still crimson, turned toward the nearest counter and put her head down on it, hiding her face in her arms. "I'm sorry," she said, muffled. "I'm not usually like this."

"You're the...single?...mother of an energetic four-year-old," Jake said, still grinning, but with genuine admiration and sympathy. "I think you're supposed to say and think adult thoughts when you get a break from parenting."

Mabs turned her head to peek at him from the corner of her elbow, eyes shining with what looked like tears of laughter. He hoped that's what they were, anyway, but given how the skin crinkled, he was pretty sure she was smiling. Mabs Brannigan giving him a hidden smile was wonderful. It felt like a secret between them, like it belonged in a comfortable space they'd already somehow built.

"I'm obviously out of practice thinking adult thoughts," she said, still into the corner of her elbow. "They didn't use to make me blush."

"I'll overlook it this time," Jake promised.

Aw.

Shush, he told the wolf. *I just met her. She doesn't need me coming on like a freight train. Even if I was looking for a relationship, which I'm not* .

Wolves weren't quite as good at rolling their eyes as dogs were, due to the eyebrow muscle dogs had developed to wrap humans around their paws. Jake's wolf still managed a pretty convincing eye roll. Jake said, *Shush,* again, as Mabs, still pink-cheeked, straightened up and rubbed her hand over her face. "Thanks. I'd usually drop that kind of thought on a girlfriend, not a nice guy I just met. And yeah, single mom. Noah's dad knows he exists, but that's about the sum total of their relationship."

"He's obviously an idiot," Jake said with feeling.

"No argument here. So," Mabs said emphatically,

"are we moving counters or what?"

"How about..." Jake went along the wall, a hand extended to run his fingertips over the boards, rapping on them occasionally. The sound changed as he hit a support column, and he tapped the counter in front of it. "How about we start by moving this one and taking the board out, and see how much space it looks like we can fill with just one board removed? If it turns out we need to move everything, you can display your Tetris skills later."

Mabs put a hand over her face, laughed, nodded, and started moving crockery.

CHAPTER 5

Mabs was prepared to kick herself for the rest of the night—possibly the rest of her life—over the *I can fit anything anywhere* comment, just like any normal, functioning adult would. Jake Rowly was really nice about it, though, and hadn't made her feel any more idiotic than she did on her own.

Which made her all the more inclined to see where he would fit with her, but that was *not* part of her game plan for the next...forever. Roughly forever. She might have time for a boyfriend at the end of forever. Until then, there was the house and Noah and her job and...and it was interesting that she'd reminded herself more of that in the past four hours than she had in the past two years combined.

Jake Rowly didn't criticize the tools she had on hand, although she could practically see him mentally comparing their quality to what he had. He didn't once assume she couldn't do something, which, after

Noah's dad, was...mind-boggling, really. Jake took her lead in moving counters and shelving into the buttery. When they'd emptied out pretty well everything but the Aga, he stood back to look at the smaller room and said, "Wow," with evident sincerity. "It's not that I didn't believe you, but I couldn't have made it fit."

"I used to rearrange the contents of our freezer, when I was a kid. You know how stuff just ends up shoved in and piled up? I always thought it was really satisfying to make it fit neatly and my mom was always amazed at how much room there was when I was done." Mabs grinned up at Jake, whose return smile made her toes curl.

Furthermore, it made other parts of her tingle, which hadn't happened in a long time, and which led right back into *I can fit anything anywhere*, a thought which Mabs absolutely refused to pursue. She refused to pursue it vividly, and with detail that lingered on those long, strong fingers, and how the size of a man's hands were said to reflect the size of his...gloves....

"You could probably make a living out of organizing freezers," Jake said with admiration. "People like people who can arrange their lives for them."

"I wouldn't know how to market myself," Mabs admitted. "Otherwise I might. I bet I could charge a lot."

"You probably could. We'll go into business," he suggested lightly. "I'll restore and renovate, you'll organize what they have into the new spaces."

"Deal," Mabs said just as lightly, and tried not to

think about how the idea actually sounded kind of wonderful.

Not that she knew Jake Rowly well enough to go into business with him, but still, at first blush, she really *liked* him. Liked him so much it was kind of alarming, in fact. But even if she didn't *like*-like him, it would be good to have more friends. She'd done pretty well for herself in that department, in the months they'd been in Virtue, but more friends was always good.

And of course there were friends, and then there were... *friends*.

Mabs did not need any *friends*, gosh darn it. Not right now. For now, Jake showing her how to remove boards without damaging the walls was enough. He said, "It's almost impossible to do this without some damage, but I've got a lot of practice," while doing it, and nodded at the ancient, not-quite-rusted nails. "Sometimes they're screwed in instead of nailed and that's easier."

He'd put his big hands over hers, guiding her through the motions to carefully remove them. His hands were warm and certain and very gentle, and he was careful to keep enough distance between their bodies to be polite, although Mabs wouldn't have minded a little more press of hips, herself. Or a lot more, for that matter. On the other hand, she really appreciated the gentlemanly effort.

He was patient, too. Where she would have given up in frustration and yanked at a board, he worked at it slowly and cautiously, removing it with a delicacy she wouldn't have expected from those big hands. She couldn't help thinking about what *else* he could do with that kind of patience, and found herself out of breath and aching with desire more than once as they worked.

Fortunately—fortunately?—there was so much to do that sometimes she forgot that the virtual stranger in her kitchen was staggeringly attractive, incredibly kind, and had a touch that set her whole body alight with need.

It turned out copper piping had been laid in between the exterior and interior walls at some point, which was great. Even Mabs could tell it was in good condition, with no leaks or damp places, as they gradually revealed it.

That job meant they spent a long time lying on the floors, gently removing boards along the whole length of the wall so they could expose the pipes for insulating. Mabs eventually rolled over onto her back, sweating, and stared at the ceiling eight feet above her. "Oh God. I'm too old to be lying on the floor for hours at a time."

"No one with purple hair is ever truly old."

Mabs lifted her head to smile at Jake, who sat up to loop his arms around his knees, holding a hammer between his hands. "Lots of old ladies have purple hair."

"That's accidental. Yours is carefully considered."

"I'd toss it to show off how carefully considered it is, but my whole body hurts too much." She put her head back down and regarded the ceiling again. "We need to take that down too, don't we? So we can insulate it?"

"Yeah. We're just gonna tackle this whole kitchen

over the weekend. You won't know it, by Monday." Jake squinted upward. "Except ideally it'll look exactly the same when we put it back together, so maybe I'm wrong about that."

Mabs chuckled, then groaned and stretched along the floor. It pulled her jeans against her crotch and reminded her of the considerable wet desire that had built up. She bit her lip, tried to think of something not-sexy, and said, "I don't know how I'm going to keep Noah out of here while we're doing all that."

"First thing we'll do is insulate the pipes and re-board the bottoms of the walls so he can't get into them," Jake suggested. "Then insulation for the exterior wall space, and *then* we'll tackle the ceiling and the piping on the inside kitchen wall. You said some of it needed replacing?"

"The faucet does. I don't know about the actual pipes." Mabs started to rise and Jake stood up to offer her a hand. He pulled her up so easily her feet nearly came off the floor, and he caught her with an arm around her waist, their bodies pressed together as she'd been imagining.

Well, maybe not *quite* as she'd been imagining, but pretty close. An apology died on Jake's lips, turning into a cautious, curious smile, as if he felt the embrace was as *right* as Mabs herself did. She tilted her chin up, the beginnings of an answer...

...and Noah burst through the door, shouting, "Mama! Mama! I had *chicken fries* for dinn— *whoa.*" He skidded to a halt, gaping at the empty kitchen, as Jake, looking guilty, released Mabs. Mabs staggered back a step, blushing, and Noah turned to her with wide eyes. "Mama, what happened here?"

Sarah, still out in the yard, yelled, "Sorry, I lost control of the whirlwind!" and came in several steps behind Noah, carrying a bag labeled with the town's best takeout burgers. Like Noah, her jaw dropped as she came through the door, and she echoed his, "Whoa. Look at how much work you've gotten done!"

Mabs, almost certain her blush had faded before Sarah arrived, and incredibly grateful for it, picked up Noah with a grin. "We're gonna insulate the walls tomorrow, like we did with the floor! What do you think, baby?"

He took in the room with a dismayed gaze. "I liked it better before."

"Aw." Mabs kissed his hair. "Me too, but it'll be back to normal in a few days."

"Okay!" Noah slithered out of her arms and barreled toward Sarah to try grabbing the takeout bag from her. "We brought dinner! Mr. Collins said it was on the house, but I don't think we should put it on the house, Mommy. That would be messy."

"And hard to get to, if we put it on the roof," Mabs agreed with a smile. "How about we eat on the porch instead? Although I hear you already had chicken fries, so maybe you don't need anything else to eat."

"*Mommy!*" Noah spoke with horrified outrage that made all the adults laugh.

Sarah said, "The porch it is," and led him out, while Mabs lingered to look over the kitchen, then at Jake.

"They're right. We did do a lot today, and I couldn't

have done it without you. Thank you, Jake. This morning I felt like everything was lost. I have some hope now."

"I felt pretty lost and out of sorts this morning myself," he admitted. "I'm not sure I even meant to come back to Virtue, honestly. I just kind of...found myself here."

"Lucky me," Mabs said softly, and meant it.

"Lucky us," he suggested, and might have said more, but Noah yelled, "Mama!" from the porch, and Mabs laughed.

"Dinner calls."

Jake, deadpan, said, "I had no idea burgers had such vocal range," and they went out to the porch together, both smiling. If someone had told her six hours earlier that she'd spend most of the afternoon and evening with a smile on her face, Mabs just wouldn't have believed them. She owed Jake Rowly a lot, just for making her feel like her life wasn't a total loss.

"I brought you curly fries," Noah announced proudly as they came onto the porch. Mabs's heart melted and she bent to kiss his hair.

"Thank you, honey. And a burger? It looks great." She sank onto the porch seat beside her son and sighed with contentment as she took the first bite of burger. Maybe, just maybe, things would work out.

CHAPTER 6

Jake was up way too early Saturday morning, with plans to lean heavily on relationships that had lain fallow since high school, over twenty years ago. One good thing about small towns, though, was there were generally two kinds of people: those who left and never came back, and those who just never left.

Cynthia Bullock was one of the latter. She'd married her high school sweetheart, inherited the family hardware store, and remembered Jake with enough fondness that she lent him the insulation blower on a previously non-existent line of credit. Her older son, who was twenty, which seemed ridiculous to Jake, helped him load it, and a pile of other renovation material, into the bed of his truck, and he arrived at the old Brannigan place just before eight in the morning.

Only after he killed the truck's engine did he think that maybe most people weren't up before eight on a Saturday, and that he would appear much too eager.

Hnf, his wolf said. *Not eager enough, if you ask me.*

I didn't. Before Jake could argue further, Noah came plowing out of the house, jumped down the porch steps, and ran full speed into the front gate separating him from the truck. "Mommy, did Auntie Sarah get a new *truck* ?"

"Sorry, Noah." Jake got out of the truck, smiling apologetically. "It's just me. I rode over with Sarah yesterday, but I've got my own truck, see? And I came over to help your mom work on the kitchen."

Noah gave him a vaguely suspicious look that dissolved into eagerness. "Mama says *I* can help. Mama! The strange man is here!" He went running back to the porch, leaving Jake bemused as the lady of the house came out, drying her hands on a dishtowel.

"I'm not *that* strange!" he called to her, hoping he sounded amusing and reassuring. "Sorry I'm so early!"

You're pretty strange, the wolf said. *For a human.*

I'm incredibly boring and normal for a shapeshifter, though.

"Well, come on in," Mabs called back. "We're always up early around here. I've got breakfast on the...floor..." His wolf-enhanced hearing caught her sighed, "Ah, man," at the end of that, as though she felt silly. In her defense—and Jake felt the impulse *to* defend her, even from herself, if necessary—they *had* taken all the furniture out of the kitchen the night before. The floor was kind of the only option.

The scent of bacon and eggs came out of the open door, and Jake's stomach rumbled. God, she was adorable, brave, determined, and also cooked? He

might need to reconsider his stance on no relationships.

Good plan, his wolf said brightly. Jake said, "Ungh,"
under his breath, swung open the front gate, and took
himself up to the house for crisp bacon and—to his
surprise—homemade bread, fresh from the oven. "This
is amazing. So you're actually a superwoman, is that it?"
he said to Mabs around a bite of butter-laden bread.

"You should see me in spandex."

This time Mabs didn't blush, but Jake coughed on
the bite of bread, tears springing to his eyes as he
wheezed around crumbs. He finally managed to say, "I
can imagine," at which Mabs gave him a smirking
wink.

The trouble was, he *could* imagine. He could *easily*
imagine the form-fitting outfit, following her curves
even more intimately than her jeans and t-shirt.

He could imagine the stretch emphasizing her
thighs, and the fabric squeezing her hips, outlining
them, and he couldn't help but notice that in his imagination she wasn't wearing any panties under the spandex, either. He could imagine the snug fit at her small
waist, and for some reason he *very clearly* imagined one
of those universally-reviled-by-women 'boob windows'
showing off a truly generous amount of cleavage.

In his imagination, the costume had a high collar
above the boob window, but cut away from her shoulders so he could see her collarbones and another hint
of her tattoos. He wasn't sure about the physics of that
in the real world, but it worked really, really well in his
imagination.

This was, he told himself shakily, probably a terrible kind of objectification, but *God*, it was hot, too. He wanted to get up for a drink of water, but he had an erection so hard he thought he might pass out if he stood up, even if he could somehow hide it from...

...from the mother of the four-year-old chowing down on breakfast across from him. Mabs being a mother wasn't a turn-off at *all*, but remembering there was a kid right there took the edge off his ardor. Thank God. "I picked up some foam pipe insulation," he said to Mabs. "I thought if I cut it to length, Noah could help installing that, since it goes down low."

The little boy brightened and a soft bloom of astonished joy rose in Mabs's face. "That's an amazing idea. Thank you for thinking of that, Jake. That's...thank you. Most people wouldn't."

"Kids like to help out," Jake said easily. He didn't know much about kids, really, but he did know they liked to do important work, just like adults did. He also knew they often got bored fast, and in fact, after breakfast was finished and Noah had put the first two or three lengths of insulation on the pipes, he lost interest and wandered off.

Mabs took over where he'd left off, while Jake reapplied the boards they'd taken out behind her. "Thanks," she said again, quietly, when Noah had gone. "Really, it means a lot that you thought of something for him to do. Kids are a nuisance and most guys don't get farther than thinking about that."

Jake glanced toward her to answer, and forgot what he'd meant to say. She was crawling down the floorboards to the next section of insulation she needed to lay, and her bottom was perfectly encased in her jeans at eye-level. The idea of just crawling over behind her and pulling her back against himself filled his mind for a moment, and got an unfortunately enthusiastic yip of approval from his wolf. His voice sounded hoarse to him as he said, "Not a lot of luck dating, then? I mean, not that it's my business, but..."

She glanced back with a wry smile and didn't seem to notice—or care, at least—that he was checking out her behind. "No, not really. I mean, who has time, for one thing, but yeah, the single mom thing is a big red flag for a lot of guys. Oh, that looks nice." She waved at what he'd put back together, and went on to finish her own work.

"Thanks." They worked in companionable silence until suddenly they'd reached the end of the pipes and walls. Jake, groaning cheerfully, got to his feet. "Wall insulation next, but I need to stretch first. Have you talked to the heritage society about the windows?"

Dismay crossed Mabs's face. "They fall in a kind of no-man's-land. They're not original, but they're old enough to have heritage value, so the heritage society would *like* me to preserve them, but they're also only single-pane, so I'm guessing they leak heat like a sieve. Not that you can put heat in a sieve, but you know what I mean."

"I do." Jake, rotating his hips and stretching his arms until he touched the ceiling, went over to study one of the 12-pane sash windows. "Well, let's be realistic. Tackling the windows isn't necessarily a job for this time of year anyway. We might have to think about it next summer."

Mabs chuckled wryly. "Planning to stay in my barn that long?"

Jake bit down the impulse to say *yes!* and said, "Or on Sarah's couch," instead.

"It'd probably be warmer than my barn." Mabs sounded concerned, and Jake's wolf said, *We have a fur coat. We'll be fine.*

Yeah, but she doesn't know that.

*Well, **tell** her,* the wolf said, exasperated.

Jake smiled. Out loud he said, "We'll worry about that when it gets colder," and to the wolf, said, *If I tell her that I come equipped with a fur coat, assuming she doesn't freak out and run away to start with, then she'll never have reason to invite me **in** to sleep.*

The wolf said, *ooooooh,* in appreciation of Jake's subtlety, and Jake's smile widened as Mabs nodded, accepting "we'll figure it out later" as an acceptable way of dealing with problems that weren't actually immediate.

Noah reappeared when they started filling the walls with insulation, his hands clamped over his ears and his eyes huge with interest. "You! Guys! Look! Like! *Monsters* !"

Jake, glancing between himself and Mabs, thought the kid wasn't wrong. They had all the necessary protective equipment—masks, eye and ear protection, gloves, long sleeves—and looked nothing like they had when Noah had last seen them. Mabs went "Raar!" and started chasing Noah around the kitchen to shrieks of laughter so loud Jake could hear them over the blower.

He turned it off and pulled his goggles up, delighted to just be part of their happy moment, even as an outsider. Once the blower was off, Noah bellowed, "What are you doing?" with roughly the same intensity he'd used before. Mabs explained it to him in normal tones, and he remembered to say, "Can I help?" in a more or less regular volume.

"Um, I don't know, honey, you need all this protective stuff we've got..." Mabs took her goggles off, though, and put them on his face for a moment, and Jake, looking to her for permission, picked Noah up so he could guide the blower into the wall for a few seconds.

"That's enough," he said after a minute. "You need all this gear, and I don't have extras, sorry. They don't come in kid sizes." The truth was Jake hadn't thought to bring them for Noah, but he was reasonably certain that he also wasn't lying about kid sizes.

A sly look crossed Noah's face and he ran off. Mabs, watching him go, says, "I bet you five dollars he comes back totally prepped."

"I wouldn't take that bet," Jake said with a smile. "Not against his mother, who must know him best."

"Smart man."

They turned the blower back on, and a few minutes later Noah arrived in swim goggles, a bandana over his face, and a superhero costume with sleeves tucked into winter gloves at least five sizes too big for him. "I'm ready!"

No one, not even his mother, could argue with his preparedness, so the next half hour or so was spent trading a small child back and forth so he could fill walls with the spray insulation. A little to Jake's surprise, Noah's intense concentration lasted until they'd filled an entire section and the next thing that had to be done was replacing boards. Everybody washed up and Mabs made an actual stack of peanut butter and jelly sandwiches while Jake carefully re-boarded the wall.

Noah finished his sandwich at about the same time Jake finished the wall, announced he was going to go be a wolf, and ran outside with no further ado. Mabs, leaning on a wall, yelled, "Be careful!" after him with the air of a parent who had no expectation of the request being honored. "You were great with him," she said to Jake. "Thanks."

"It's not hard. He seems like a pretty great kid."

"He is." Mabs made a face. "Except when he's not."

Jake laughed. "To be fair, that could be said about all of us."

"So, so true. Well, we made pretty good progress this morning, even though he was helping us. Think we can get the rest of the front kitchen wall done this afternoon?"

"With time left to spare," Jake promised, but Mabs didn't look like she'd heard him. She pushed off the wall and went to the window, frowning through it with her sandwich forgotten in her hand.

"Who the hell," she said, almost conversationally. "I don't know that car." Her expression turned grim and

Jake went to join her at the window as the pleasantry dropped from her voice. "Dammit, I never said he could come by. Excuse me." She brushed past Jake to the front door, and he looked out the window to see Preston Cole, high school bully and—according to the emblem on his car—present-day realtor, walking through the front gate.

CHAPTER 7

"Ms. Brannigan? I'm Preston Cole." Cole let himself through the front gate like he had every right to, which set Mabs's teeth on edge. He had the look of an aging high school football star, with thinning hair, broad shoulders, and a bit of a paunch that his suit hid pretty well. His tie matched a yellow lapel handkerchief.

"I figured." Mabs gestured at his car, with the company name emblazoned on it. "I didn't expect to see you, Mr. Cole." She was absolutely certain her tone conveyed *and I didn't want to, either*, but it was already clear that Preston Cole was the kind of man who only heard 'no' when he was the person saying it.

"I heard about your troubles with the contractor," Cole said. "I was hoping if I came up here in person, you could see the sense in selling now, before you've put any time or eff..." His tone changed entirely as the door opened and closed again behind Mabs. "...Jake?"

"Preston." Jacob Rowly came down the steps to stand just behind Mabs. "Long time no see."

"I hadn't heard you were back in town." Cole didn't sound particularly delighted about it.

"Just blew in," Jake said easily. "Congrats on the real estate business."

"Oh..." Cole looked over his shoulder, eyebrows furrowing as if he hadn't realized his car would tell anybody anything, then frowned back at Jake. "Thanks. What're you doing here?"

"Ms. Brannigan has hired me to help restore her place." Jake produced a card from his back pocket and walked it up to Cole while Mabs watched, certain she was witnessing some kind of old high school rivalry playing out decades after the fact. Both men had that air about them, as if re-establishing old marks in a pissing contest.

Cole took Jake's card and read it like he couldn't help himself. "Jacob Rowly, Carpentry & Restorations, huh? This old place isn't worth the effort, Jake, you know that."

To Mabs's surprise, Jake stepped back until he was behind her again. "Obviously I disagree, Preston, but even if I didn't, it's Ms. Brannigan's house and Ms. Brannigan's choice."

"I appreciate your interest, Mr. Cole," Mabs said, recognizing when she'd been tagged back in. "And I won't lie, the price you quoted is life-changing. But so is this old farmstead," she said a little more quietly. "In a whole different way, maybe, but it's what I want."

"Ms. Brannigan, I don't understand. You could *buy* a

whole new turnkey farm for what you're being offered." Cole hadn't come any farther down the walk since Jake had joined Mabs in front of the porch, but she was certain he'd be up close and trying to intimidate her if she was alone.

And even though knowing that made her mad, she also still couldn't help but smile a little bit, kind of incredulously. "A new farmstead wouldn't have belonged to my family for two hundred years, Mr. Cole. People wouldn't give directions by it, or mention its name like an old baronial title. It wouldn't be 'the Old Brannigan Place'."

"Six months ago you didn't even know anyone in your family owned an old farmstead!"

Mabs gave him the best edged smile she had at her disposal. "I know. Funny how emotion works, isn't it? Six months ago I didn't know it even existed, and now I want very much for it to keep existing, as a home for me and my son. So I won't be selling. But thank you for your interest, Mr. Cole." She turned her back on the realtor, catching Jake's eye, and didn't quite let herself exhale a sigh of relief as the carpenter followed her like a liege lord's sworn man.

The front door closed behind them, and a few seconds later, the front gate banged shut and the hollow thud of a car door closing echoed up the walk before Cole drove away.

Only then did Mabs sag against the door, her heart rate suddenly soaring. Nausea boiled in her belly and she muttered, "Crackers," before pushing past Jake into the kitchen, where she pulled a packet of Saltines off a cupboard shelf and ate two in a single bite.

Then her mouth was too dry to eat anything, or talk, or even breathe, so, coughing, she went to the sink and sucked a handful of water straight from the faucet without getting a glass. After a moment Jake appeared with a glass, offered it to her, and stepped back once she'd taken it.

He really did need to write a *How to be a Better Boyfriend* book, she thought. Men were always trying to fix things. Noah's father had always made her feel like *she* couldn't possibly fix anything. But Jake just gave her what she needed and got out of the way. She'd never liked any guy in her entire life more than she liked Jake Rowly, right then. Not even in a jump-his-bones kind of way, although that too, but just...appreciating him.

Her stomach settled as she drank the water and turned the faucet off. Only then did she finally dare to try speaking, and the first words out of her mouth were, "Thanks. That kind of guy only listens a woman if there's a man around to back her up."

"Funny, that's exactly what he was like in high school, too. I didn't mean to butt in."

Mabs turned toward him, shaking her head. "No, seriously, you were great. He knew I wasn't alone so he wasn't gonna get pushy, but you weren't pushy either. I really appreciate it."

"I think you'd have rousted him on your own."

"Probably, but it was easier with backup." A zing of longing shot through Mabs. Not for Jake specifically, although—again—that too, but for a partner. For somebody who would be there like Jake had just been. It wasn't fair to count on him in particular. He'd been there now, but she was certain he wasn't planning on becoming the man-around-the-house for a single mom and her kid. Still, it made her realize how much she'd like to have *someone*.

Either way, it wasn't something she could deal with right now. "Okay. That's over. Let's move on, huh? I need another drink of water and then we can get back to the insulation."

"Sounds like a plan. And look, Mabs? If he comes back and you need backup again, just say the word. I'll follow your lead, but don't be shy about asking. I'd like to help."

A real smile blossomed in her, and she looked over her shoulder at Jake as she reached to turn the water on again. "Thank you. I hope I don't have to take you up on it, but I will if he comes sniffing around again."

She filled her glass, turned the faucet back off, and the whole thing came apart in her hands, spraying water everywhere.

To Mabs's never-ending gratification, she was not the only person in the room who screamed like an overwrought four-year-old. Jake shrieked and kicked the insulation blower—which was not meant for kicking—toward the door. Mabs shrieked and shoved her hands over the spraying faucet, which made things much, much worse until she managed to push her way through the pressure to clamp her palms against the pipe.

"Turn the water off! Turn it off turn it off turn it off!"

Jake rushed toward her, scrambling at the pieces of dissolved faucet, trying to find a place to crank it back off again. Mabs howled, "Beneath the sink!" She sucked her gut in and stuck her butt out, trying to make room between herself and the edge of the sink for Jake to open a cupboard door beneath her. He pulled at one of the doors, scraping her thighs, and she yelled, "Or at the shut-off valve! If I take my hands off this the whole kitchen's gonna be ruined!"

Jake blurted, "I'm sorry," lifted her up at the hips, opened the cupboard, and put her back down again before ducking down to check the pipes. A bubble of laughter pushed up inside her chest. He'd lifted her so *easily*, with such strength and confidence, and she could think of all sorts of much more wonderful things he could be doing with that strength than getting her out of the way of a burst faucet.

The bubbling laughter exploded as Jake, frustrated, cried, " *Shit*, there's no stopcock!"

Mabs shrieked, "That's what she said!" and began absolutely weeping with laughter, which made it incredibly hard to hold the water down. A bellow of laughter escaped Jake, too, and he climbed up from his knees to put his hands over hers on the burst faucet.

"Do you kn—stop that! Stop that!" Giggles overtook them both and he ducked his head, trying to control himself. "Do you know where the shut-off valve is?"

"Yeah, yeah, of course, it's—"

"No, no, just go, I'll hold this, go go go!"

Mabs pulled her hands out from under Jake's, wiped them—pointlessly—on her soaking wet jeans, and ran from the kitchen to throw herself into the cellar, where the pipes ran. She clobbered her head on a floor joist, but got the water shut off with a few hard twists of the wrench that Aunt Doris had obviously left down there for exactly that purpose. Mabs had intended to move it, but now she understood why it was there, and it would never, ever be 'put away'. A moment later she crawled back out, holding her head, crying now with both pain and laughter, and staggered back into the kitchen. "It's gonna splash everywhere when you take your hands off, but the water's off. Oh, let me get towels..."

She ran from the room again and grabbed a pile of them from the basket she needed to take to the local laundromat, then ran back in to thrust them over Jake's hands before he withdrew them from the broken faucet. He put his hands back on top of hers, on top of the faucet, as soon as he'd extracted them from below the towels.

Water soaked through the towels instantly, spilling into the sink and over its edges, down the back kitchen wall, before the pressure in the pipes subsided. They stared at each other, wide-eyed, and at the towels, for long seconds before either of them dared take their hands away.

The towels shifted with the changing weight and both Mabs and Jake flinched like a chest-burster was about to jump out at them. Nothing more exciting happened, though, and as one, they slid down the sink front to the kitchen floor, gasping and giggling with relief. Jake, surveying the floor and far wall, said, "There's hardly any damage. It missed the insulation, and the walls are just damp."

Mabs wiped her eyes, giggling. "Thank goodness, because look at *us*." Her t-shirt stuck to her body and her jeans had that awful gritty feeling denim got when it was wet, and Jake...

She'd know he had a strong build, but a wet t-shirt really made the definition of his muscles clear. Water dribbled down his jaw and into the hollow of his throat, where it tangled in the first hints of chest hair, and she could follow that line of darkness all the way down to his navel, where the wet shirt rumpled over the top of his jeans. Dark blue jeans, almost black with water, that clung to his thighs and knees. Mabs would have said he couldn't be any more beautiful than he'd been when she first saw him, but it turned out wet t-shirts were even better.

A sigh escaped her, and she tore her gaze away from the handsome carpenter to thump the back of her head lightly against the cupboard they both leaned against. "Well, that's twice in a row today that I'm really glad you were here. That would've been a total disaster without a second person—a second *grown-up* —here."

"On the other hand, you probably wouldn't have had the walls exposed and an insulation blower in the middle of the room if I hadn't been here, so it wouldn't have been as bad?"

Mabs pushed her shoulder against his. "I'm trying to say thank you."

"You're welcome." Jake bumped his head against the cupboard, too, and studied the ceiling. "So...faucets next?"

A high unhappy laugh escaped Mabs. "I guess so. It was supposed to be the walls and ceiling first. You said plumbing's not your specialty."

"And it's not, but needs must, and besides..." He nudged his shoulder against hers in return, smiling when she looked at him. "Besides, I'm good at following instructions, and the internet is *full* of instructions for this kind of thing. We might as well put our amateur-hour expert construction hats on and go for it."

"Is it worth it?" The smallness of her voice surprised Mabs. "Preston Cole's offering half a million dollars for this old place. He's right. I could buy a new place and have money left over."

"Half a...whew." Jake exhaled and fell silent a few long moments, like he was really thinking about what she'd said. "That's a lot of money. But, Mabs...everything you said to Preston was true. Money can't buy the history in this house. That's worth a lot. More than money, in its way."

"Yeah, but..." Mabs closed her eyes. "History can't buy new faucets."

"Ah, well, we got those on credit along with the insulation blower." Jake stood, offering Mabs a hand, and she took it with a rueful smile.

"I've made some friends since we moved here, but

not 'local-hardware-credit-line' friends. What'd you do, lean on old high school prom dates?"

"Something like that, yeah. Anyway, we'll need to find a plumber to check out all the pipes before we start adding interior insulation, but we ought to be able to handle a new faucet, anyway. Deal?" Although he'd pulled her to her feet and released her hand, Jake offered his hand again, this time to shake.

"Deal, but how about I get us some dry towels first so we can, uh, dry off, oh, God, I'm so good with the language...." Mabs shook Jake's hand, but then put her face in her hands and sighed. She honestly hadn't been so verbally inept around a guy since like 9th grade. She'd ask what was *wrong* with her, but: hot wet guy doing handiwork in her kitchen. That pretty much covered it.

At least Jake didn't sound like he noticed, or minded. "Good idea. I was thinking I'd have to go hang my shirt on the line."

Mabs, imagining hot wet *half-naked* guy doing handiwork in her kitchen, kicked herself all the way to the towels.

CHAPTER 8

Noah Brannigan came running back in, dirtier than before but drawn by the commotion. Jake, surprised, realized how little time had actually passed between Noah's departure and the faucet explosion. "Were you guys screeching? You shouldn't screech, Mama, it's very annoying. Oh no! Did you spill? A *big* spill," he said in wonder as he took in the mess in the kitchen.

Mabs agreed, "A big spill," and scooped her son up to bury her face in his hair. Jake had a little pang of—not envy, exactly. He wasn't jealous of a four-year-old. He just kinda wished Mabs could turn to *him* for comfort, too.

Although at the moment he was damp and probably smelled faintly of wet dog, so maybe not.

*Wet **wolf**,* his wolf said, offended. *And you do **not**.*

No, I know. Jake smiled at himself a little, and more at the wolf, and most of all, at Mabs and Noah. *But it was funny.*

The wolf reluctantly conceded it *might* have been funny, and Jake went out to the truck to get parts for the faucet while Mabs finished explaining to Noah what had happened in the kitchen. The little boy hung around to watch them fix it, and the kitchen floor had mostly dried out by the time they had, a little while later.

Both adults stared nervously at it, though, instead of turning it on. "The thing is," Mabs said, "I'm afraid the faucet was the same age as the pipes, and if we turn it all back on, the whole water system is just going to explode. We could...leave it off until I can get a plumber in..." She made a face that wrinkled her nose. Jake was taken with the nearly overwhelming urge to kiss that nose in response.

I would!

You, Jake pointed out, *are a canine. People expect dogs they've just met might give them kisses. Not so much humans.* Aloud, he said, "You can't just be without water until you get a plumber in."

A little smile crept across Mabs's lips. "Did you know this place is on well water? The old hand pump out back still works. It's not ideal, but we're not going to die of thirst."

Childhood memory swept Jake in a rush that left him almost laughing. "I remember that thing. We used to run around to the back for water and Ms. Brannigan would make a fuss, yelling about kids on her land, and then she'd give us cookies."

"Oh!" Mabs pressed a hand to her heart, which was tricky, since she hadn't put Noah down yet. "Oh, that's wonderful. I really don't know anything about her at all. Thank you." Her eyes shone as she smiled at Jake. "Thank you for giving me a little part of her."

Noah, less sentimental, squirmed down and grabbed Jake's hand. "C'mon, I'll show you the pump, it's AWESOOOOOME!" He bodily dragged Jake toward the back of the house. Mabs, laughing, followed along behind them, but it wasn't the old water pump that made Jake slow in astonishment as they exited the back door.

Old Ms. Brannigan had kept a patch of the land clear out there, but Mabs had taken the whole thing down to topsoil and grown a quarter-acre garden on it. She'd reclaimed stones from somewhere and laid out paths through the vegetable patches, and a path of pale pebbles led in a pretty curve toward the water pump. Behind him, sheepishly, Mabs said, "I always wanted to garden."

"This is amazing." Jake turned to her with genuine awe. "This is amazing, Mabs. You've done a huge amount of work out here. I mean, I haven't seen it in years, but..."

She smiled shyly, which made him want to scoop her up and spin her around. "It was a lot of work, but it was quieter than banging around in the house, so I could do it after Noah went to sleep."

"Like a garden fairy," Noah informed Jake.

"Only because I'm short," Mabs replied, and Noah laughed as he ran to hug her.

"You're not short! You're mommy-sized!"

Mabs laughed, too, and hugged him. Jake, smiling,

went to discover an old, well-sealed wooden bucket behind the pump. He rinsed it, primed the pump, and grinned as Noah ran over to put his hands into the sudden rush of well water. Jake washed his own hands in it, then cupped them and drank the teeth-achingly cold water and shook himself all over when he'd finished. "Best water on earth."

"I don't know what it is about the pump's water, when it's all the same, but...yeah." Mabs came over for a drink, too, before giving a rueful little sigh. "I guess I'd better go call around for a plumber. Friggin' *Chad* was supposed to be taking care of all of that." She made strangling motions with her hands, and Noah stepped up, his blue eyes worried.

"Are you mad, Mommy? I know we're supposed to use our words, but I thought of something *better* to make you feel better."

Mabs's hands relaxed as her eyebrows elevated at her son's guileless expression. "Oh yeah? What's that?"

"A *puppy*."

Mabs threw her head back and laughed out loud. It made a beautiful line of her throat, and the creases around her mouth and eyes as she laughed and laughed and laughed were the most kissable, wonderful things Jake had ever seen. She finally wiped her eyes, still giggling, and said, "A *puppy*, huh?" to Noah, who nodded vigorously. "I'm not sure a puppy will help me get the pipes fixed, honey, but I'll keep it in mind."

Noah squinted suspiciously, but then nodded as if satisfied the seed had been planted. He ran off to play, and Mabs was still grinning when she turned to Jake. "Know any puppies who are handy with plumbing?"

His wolf's tail drooped. *We're only good with wood.*

Jake croaked, "Ask Sarah. She'll know who to talk to," and said *'We're only good with wood'?!?* to his wolf.

What ? the wolf asked, baffled. *What?*

Explaining double-entendres to a wolf proved beyond him. Jake, still hoarsely, said, "And look, if Sarah's contact turns out to be an old high school buddy, let me call them for you?", and tried to keep his mind far, far out of the gutter. It didn't work, but he tried.

"I'll think about," Mabs promised.

Jake went to start taking boards off the interior kitchen walls, revealing pipes that even he could recognize weren't in great condition, while Mabs called Sarah, who gave her a name. Mabs checked to see if Jake knew them, and he didn't, so she called them herself, and just before dinner a kid who looked about 17 and pimply came over to look at the exposed pipes.

The estimate he gave made Mabs have to sit down for a bit, although he did say the current pipes wouldn't explode if they turned the water back on, which was something. Jake followed him back out of the house to ask if he needed any work done in trade, and the kid said he'd talk to his boss, and that was something, too. Jake gave him a card and went back into the house, where Mabs was staring at the open walls of her kitchen.

"We don't need the whole house done at once, even if that'd probably be cheapest," she said a little dully.

"But we really need the kitchen to be usable, and if I'm getting pipes done then I should get a more functional bathroom in place. We've been using the one in the buttery wing at night, but it's awful and I don't want to have to use an outhouse in the winter if we can avoid it. But that means rearranging the upstairs. Or down-stairs. Both. To make room for bathrooms. And that costs a lot of money. Crap. Crap, crap, crap." She sat on the floor, her head in her hands, and Jake came to crouch nearby.

"This is what I *am* good at, though," he offered quietly. "You tell me where you want the bathrooms, I can build that space for you, upstairs and down. It'd be good to have functional plumbing before winter hits, right? And then we'll move on to the next part. If I keep busy I'll get to the roof before the snow comes."

"Jake..." Mabs lifted her head with the tone and expression of someone who was going to object, but instead she closed her eyes and, very quietly, said, "Thank you."

"If it helps, you can think of this as being my local portfolio project," Jake offered. "If I'm gonna stick around Virtue, I'll need work, and people like to be able to see what a carpenter's done."

"Actually, that does make me feel better." Mabs gave him a little nod, then exhaled noisily. "So, uh, wanna see where I was thinking of putting the bathrooms?"

Jake offered her a hand up again. He liked doing that, liked the momentary chance to hold her hand. Liked the warmth of their fingers touching, and the breath he could take of her scent. He liked being with her, which was a lot for a man who didn't think he wanted romance. "You know what? I'd love to see where you want to put the bathrooms."

By the next evening the entire house was a wreck. Jake had stayed late Saturday night, and arrived early again on Sunday morning, enduring Sarah's teasing in the brief time he'd been at her place to sleep on her couch. Mabs cleared out the old birthing room downstairs so she and Noah could share it while interior walls got moved around to accommodate bathrooms both upstairs and down. Sawdust and old boards were everywhere, including up Jake's nose and embedded deep in his hair. Well, the sawdust was, anyway, and maybe a few splinters. Not so much with the boards.

It didn't matter. He couldn't remember ever being happier. The work was hard and hot and sweaty, and he wasn't getting paid for it, but he honestly didn't care. Being near Mabs Brannigan and her funny, brash little boy lightened his heart in a way he hadn't thought was possible. He was, he realized, *dying* for Mabs to ask if he really did want to stay in the barn.

He had never wanted to stay in a barn more in his life, and he'd been the kind of kid who thought that was an exciting way to spend a summer night. But he couldn't ask, because he didn't want to be pushy.

So it came as a huge relief, after dinner, both of them sprawled on the porch to cool down and watch Noah in the yard, when Mabs said, "So...I literally can't offer you a place in the house because there isn't one, but...did you want to check out the barn? I know it's crazy, but..."

"It's the best kind of crazy I can imagine," Jake promised, then hoped he hadn't overdone it. Fortunately, Mabs just smiled, got up, and stretched before jogging down the steps and off toward the barn. Jake watched her t-shirt creep up to reveal a peek of her belly as she stretched, and for a minute had a hard time remembering how to make his legs work so he could get up and follow her.

The barn, which lay a comfortable amble away from the house, was in startlingly good condition. Jake cast Mabs a surprised look and she said, "I know, right? I seriously considered *us* living in here. Sarah said a rancher rented it a while back and fixed it all up to keep his horses warm over a winter. It's even got electricity and space heaters, so you'd be warm enough, I think?"

"I run warm anyway," Jake promised, since that was safer than mentioning his built-in fur coat. "I'd love to stay out here, Mabs. I'll stay at Sarah's tonight and pick up a sleeping pallet and some blankets in the morning and it'd be great. Are you sure?"

"I am if you are. I wish I could pay you, but..."

Jake shook his head. "You're giving me a roof to sleep under and a job I'm good at to do, one that will make a big difference in somebody's life. What else are we here for, if not to make each other's lives a little better?"

Her gaze softened into something he didn't dare

imagine a name for. "Yeah. Yeah. It's nice to meet people who think that way. Thank you, Jake. Let's get you settled in here, and we can..." Her face fell. "I can't help in the morning. I've got a shift at the restaurant."

"No problem, that's your job. Fixing this place up is mine. Do you need somebody to watch Noah?" He was surprised at how much he hoped the answer was 'yes', but she shook her head.

"No, he comes with me and goes to the library when it opens. You wouldn't be able to get anything done with him underfoot, anyway. Trust me," Mabs added wryly.

Jake, more softly than he'd intended, said, "I do," and excused himself to head out to Sarah's for the last time.

IT SEEMED like most of Virtue stopped by the diner that day, eager to talk about how Jake Rowly was back in town and living out at the Old Brannigan Place with the New Brannigan Family. Mabs gave up on saying *near, not with!* after about the thirteenth time, figuring it would seem like the lady protested too much. Even Preston Cole, in his nice suit with its sharply-ironed pocket handkerchief, came in to listen to the gossip, and clicked his tongue in disappointment at Mabs.

"I'd still like you to consider the offer, Ms. Brannigan. It's a lot of money."

"*So* much money," she agreed, but shrugged. "Thanks, but no. I really do want to keep the place."

"Well, it don't make sense to me," he said, playing up

a drawl he didn't really have, "so you keep the offer in mind, won't you?" He waved on his way out, and Mabs exhaled noisily.

"Persistent, isn't he," she said to nobody in particular, and got a general mumble of agreement from the diner's patrons.

Sarah dropped Noah back off at the diner just before Mabs's shift ended, and every time somebody mentioned the farm, he announced that Mr. Growly was helping and everybody else should come help too.

Mabs hushed him every time, looking apologetic, but she got a lot of smiles, and more than one promise to drop by and see if they could be of help. To Mabs's astonishment, there were a couple of casual friends *at* the house when they arrived home, doing the kind of grunt work that fell within Mabs's skill set, just in greater numbers.

Noah was thrilled, and ran around 'helping', giving orders, and generally getting underfoot while Mabs tried to ride herd on him and give Jake her thanks. "We're just getting started," he promised her. "Just you wait."

The helpers peeled off around dinner time, and Mabs got Noah into bed approximately on time, which was as good as it ever got. Jake went to wash up and came back to the house for a few minutes after bedtime, a smile embedded on his handsome face. "Plumber says he can squeeze the bathrooms in as soon as I've got the space roughed out. Probably over the weekend, at no extra cost."

"I have no idea how you're charming everybody

into this, but I appreciate it," Mabs said with simple honesty. "There's been more done here in the past three days than all summer."

"Give me until the end of the week," Jake said with a wink, and excused himself. Mabs lingered on the porch, watching him walk away and appreciating every step of the view. Then, suddenly realizing she was exhausted even if she hadn't been doing all that much actual renovating herself, she went and crawled into bed with Noah, who kicked her, then nestled up like a warm lump and soothed her to sleep.

Every day of the week flew by like that: a diner full of people gossiping about Mabs's new tenant, Preston Cole dropping by to try nagging Mabs into selling after all, a handful of acquaintances showing up at the house to help so they had an excuse to check out Jake Rowly's return, and falling into bed after a few minutes of quiet talk with the gorgeous carpenter.

It felt natural, and calming, and kind of wonderful. There were still so many things to deal with, but Mabs couldn't remember the last time she'd gone to bed every night happy, instead of with her stomach clenched with worry about how she was going to get through the next day.

Noah woke up early on Saturday, whispered, "Mama, can I watch some videos?" in stentorian tones, and crept off to let her sleep in a little while longer when she mumbled something that he could interpret as a 'yes.'

What felt like only seconds later, he came in to report, in an equally loud whisper, that he had made his *own* breakfast *and* cleaned up the milk so she didn't need to worry about it or get up. Mabs weighed the likelihood of that, pulled the pillow over her head, and hoped for a few more minutes of sleep.

"Mama," Noah said a while later, his little voice awed, "Mama, a *party* is here."

"Whuuh?" Mabs lurched out of bed and stumbled to the window, staring into their front yard.

The plumber was pulling up, which meant she'd slept until nearly ten. That seemed impossible, and definitely meant Noah had, in some fashion, fed himself.

But more than that, behind the plumber and parked in various places along her driveway were at least a dozen other vehicles, out of which an honestly astonishing number of people were emerging. A lot of them were carrying tools, or tool belts, or food. Mabs blinked a few times, croaked, "Oh crud," and threw herself from the window toward some clothes.

She got to the front door, mostly dressed, by the time the first neighbors knocked, and the next half hour was spent greeting people, Tetris-ing food into the fridge, and wishing she'd had time to brush her teeth. As soon as each person dropped off whatever they were carrying, they went off to have a job assigned to them. Mabs heard Sarah's voice carrying through the house, and, jacked up on adrenaline, went to find the busybody librarian.

"Mabs!" Sarah yelled cheerfully. "I've been here for an hour, you slug-a-bed! You look great!"

"I look like I'm wearing pajama bottoms and no

bra," Mabs disagreed. "Sarah, what's going on? Did you do this?"

"Honestly, I think Noah did it. He's been telling everybody, and I mean *everybody*, at the library that they should come over on Saturday to help with the house now that 'Mr. Growly' is there to do a lot of big work. And really, who can resist that kid?"

Mabs looked toward the front of the house, where she could hear Noah caroling suggestions to the plumbers, and shook her head. "Nobody. He's going to conquer the world if he survives to adulthood."

"Which you're doing an excellent job of ensuring happens," Sarah reassured her. "Speaking of which, he's talked Mrs. Knutson into one of the husky puppies from her dog's new litter. She has the sense to not just show up with a dog, but she wanted me to ask what you thought. *I* think she's desperate to find good homes for them."

"Oh my God. No, that would be crazy. Except it'd be so good for Noah, too. Give him somebody to play with. Oh, God." Mabs scrunched her face. "Huskies are a lot of work, aren't they?"

"High energy," Sarah agreed. "Just like Noah."

"I can't decide if that's a selling point or not. Okay, I'll text Mrs. Knutson later with a decision. Ugh. Um. Yeah. I have to think about that a little bit."

"Of course you do. And in the meantime, I was gonna have people start clearing out the rooms on this side of the house, if you want?"

"That would be amazing." Mabs looked around,

feeling like she had whiplash. "Especially if they did it with, uh..."

"Sensitivity?" Sarah suggested. "I've got an archivist degree and answer to the Virtue Historical Society. I won't let them throw anything important away. What about the wing behind the buttery?"

"I don't think we can throw it all away," Mabs said regretfully. "Too heavy." She grinned as Sarah elbowed her. "If people want to start clearing it out that would be incredible. I'd kind of just...given up on the idea of it for now."

"Well, you've got twenty people with more on the way because everybody wants to gawk at Jake, so we might as well take advantage of them. *And* there are a bunch of kids here already to play with Noah, so they'll keep themselves out from underfoot. Mostly."

Mabs, stunned, said, "I'm gonna...I'm gonna go put a bra on..." and left the back room, wandering out to walk straight into Jake Rowly. She actually bounced off him, and he caught her shoulders to keep her from falling. Mabs said, "Ow," and crossed an arm across her unsupported chest.

Jake's gaze followed her movement, and then, to her not-so-secret delight, the carpenter blushed bright pink and yanked his attention to the much-safer ceiling rafters. "Um. I'm sorry. Are you all right?"

"Yep. Yep. Ow, but yep. Just wasn't expecting to walk into something solid while going commando."

His eyes skittered back to hers, then away again, his blush still intact. "Is, uh, that what you call it? When you don't wear a bra? Commando? I always thought that was no underwear."

"Bras are underwear," Mabs pointed out, grinning. He was trying so hard not to stare, which was adorable. It wasn't like free-range boobs under a t-shirt were really all that exciting. Uncomfortable, yes. Exciting, not so much. At least, not from her perspective, and she decided she'd better keep her eyes high and not see how exciting it might be from Jake's.

Except then it was really hard to look anywhere but down. Mabs fixed her attention firmly on his hairline and tried not to blush. "And honestly, I don't know, I never thought about it until just this second. Jake, look at all these people!"

He stopped looking embarrassed and lit up instead. "I know! I know a couple guys from shop class back in high school and they're handy, so we're gonna get up on the roof and get busy. We've got insulation to lay, so that'll help keep the house warm when it gets colder. We'll have this old part of the house snug before winter, Mabs."

"I'm going to have to sell a kidney to pay for all of this," she whispered, "but thank you, Jake."

His smile, soft and gentle, held a little teasing, too. "This is a barn-raising, Mabs. Small towns pull together when somebody needs them. You're part of Virtue, now."

Tears stung the inside of Mabs's nose. She nodded, smiled weakly, and ran upstairs to finish getting dressed before she made a complete fool of herself in front of Jake Rowly.

CHAPTER 9

It didn't matter that Jake Rowly wasn't interested in a relationship, or didn't think anybody in Virtue suited him for one, because Mabs didn't have time to date until the heat death of the universe *anyway.* She reminded herself of that while they were working together most evenings over the next several weeks, but during the day she hardly had time to think at all, even about Jake's brilliant blue eyes and his equally brilliant smile.

Fantasies, she thought, were for people who weren't exhausted all the time. The only reason she found room for them at all was that she would have been ten times *more* exhausted if it hadn't been for Jake, who took over the house restoration like it was his life's blood. The oldest part of the house took shape under his careful, thoughtful work. Mabs came home, night after night, to the roof being finished, the plumbing being updated, and even, after a brief discussion about the financial viability, the windows being redone.

His willingness to work for so little return gave Mabs time to focus on Noah, and on work, the latter of which she desperately needed to do if she was ever going to pay Jake *anything*. Not that he seemed to care, but Mabs did. Being beholden to good-looking men was hardly ever a good idea, maybe especially for single mothers who couldn't deny they'd like a little affection in their lives.

But, she reminded herself *again*, there wasn't time for that, so she got up every morning, packed Noah up with her, and headed out to the diner while Jake put her house back together. Sarah always asked for a bit of gossip when Mabs dropped Noah off at the library, like there was a passionate affair going on at the Old Brannigan Place instead of two adults so busy with their work they hardly had time to talk to each other. Mabs disappointed her every day, but also left the library with a smile.

That smile stayed in place until she walked into the diner to find Preston Cole, with his well-cut suit, his affected pocket handkerchief—today's was sky blue—and his smarmy football hero face, waiting for her in one of the booths. "Ms. Brannigan. Nice to see you again. How's the renovation going?"

"The restoration's going pretty well, thanks." Mabs put a little emphasis on the second word, having learned from Sarah that historical societies liked restorations, not renovations. "Keeping Mr. Rowly busy. What can I get you?"

He placed his order and she went away, wishing somebody else was available to take over Cole's table.

There wasn't, though, not unless she wanted to recruit the boss, so when Preston's order came up Mabs brought it over with a brief smile. She was about to retreat without any further interaction when he said, "So if your contractor ran out with your money, how are you paying Jake?" His smarmy smile slid right into a nasty leer.

Mabs, carrying a water glass for another table, tightened her fingers around it. "I don't see how that's any of your business, Mr. Cole. Can I get you anything else with your breakfast?"

"You know you can't pay your mortgage with what you're paying Rowly with, right?" Cole's gaze ran over her whole body, lasciviously, and Mabs, knuckles white around the water glass now, reminded herself she couldn't pay the mortgage without a *job*.

Not that a house that had been in the family for two centuries had a mortgage, but that kind of wasn't the point. She gritted her teeth in a smile, said, "Let me know if you need anything," and brought the water to the other table, where Judge Owens was sitting with her teenage daughter Robin.

Behind her, Cole said, "I can see something I need," loudly enough to be heard around the whole diner. Mabs didn't need to glance over her shoulder to know he was looking at *her*. "You have any problems with that mortgage, Ms. Brannigan, you come to me. I'd be glad to make some sort of *arrangement*."

The judge's daughter, who was, Mabs thought, 17 and a senior in high school, looked from Mabs to Cole, then at her mother. "I'm gonna go use the bathroom,

Mom, do you want like another orange juice when I come back?"

Mabs, grateful for any other topic of conversation, said, "Oh, I can get tha—" as Robin got up. Mabs took a step toward the counter, about to get the juice, and the judge said, "So is Noah excited about Halloween, Mabs?"

"What?" Mabs blinked back at the judge, who came by her grandmotherly vibe honestly; she had six other children, the oldest of whom had kids older than Noah. Mabs thought she looked like Mrs. Claus, assuming Mrs. Claus ran a tight ship and brooked no fools. Which she probably did, to be fair. "Oh, God. So excited. He's gonna be Captain America. Actually, he already is, all the kids have been wearing their costumes to the library all week and they're adorable. And there's a whole town-wide trick-or-treating event on Saturday afternoon, right? That's how it works here?"

"There's a whole carnival," the judge said. "Starts at about ten, wraps up at four, and anybody who's left standing goes trick-or-treating after that. I hope we'll see you there. You and Jake both."

Mabs smiled. "I swear I'm not keeping him on a leash. Thanks, we'll be there. But let me get you that orange juice, Ju—"

Across the diner, Robin Owens had already gotten the glass of juice, and as she made her way back to her mother's table, tripped. A girlish shriek cut through the air, followed by an outraged, mannish bellow as the entire contents of the juice glass splashed onto Preston Cole's face and chest.

Robin cried, "Oh my God!" in what sounded like genuine horror while her mother leaped up to see if Robin was all right. "I'm fine!" Robin cried. "I just tripped on my shoelaces! Gosh, what a mess! Look what I've done!"

Preston snarled and stormed out, and every ounce of contrition drained from Robin, leaving her with a glow of self-satisfaction while her mother tried not to smirk. They both came back to their table, and Robin sat with her feet dangling off the side of the booth seat, where Mabs could see them easily. "I guess I should have let you get that juice after all, Ms. Brannigan."

Mabs, struggling not to smile, said, "Why don't I get it for you now? On the house. And thank you," she added softly, because Robin was wearing pretty, ballet-style flats.

Flats that didn't have a shoelace in sight.

Robin winked, her mother smirked again, and Mabs went through the rest of her shift with a light heart.

SHE CAME HOME STILL CHEERFUL, feeling as though she belonged in Virtue more than she'd ever belonged anywhere. That would have been enough, but she found Jake standing in the hallway, hands on his hips and a thoughtful expression on his face as he studied the half of the house they hadn't touched yet. "You know, snow's not due for weeks yet..."

"I did know that," said Mabs, who had not known that. A waft of wonderful scent came from the kitchen and she got distracted from asking, "So what does that mean," and said, "Oh my God, Jake, did you cook? What did you cook? It smells incredible," instead. She poked her head into the kitchen, where Wolf raised his head from beneath the table, then scrambled toward the door in search of his boy.

Noah, traipsing in behind Mabs, yelled, "WOLFIE!" and the two of them ran outdoors, where, experience told Mabs, they would remain until one or both of them was too hungry to stay away anymore. She looked after them with a smile, then arched her eyebrows at Jake, who had ignored the commotion in favor of continuing to study the unrestored half of the house.

"I went fishing this morning. Didn't catch anything, so I came in and made chili. I was thinking I haven't done much with the dining room, but we've been eating at the kitchen table anyway, and the dining room is interior work I could deal with after it snows. I could get quite a bit of work done on the roof over here before then, though."

"Oh, thank goodness," Mabs said with feeling. Jake looked at her in surprise, and she waved her hands. "You went fishing. You did something that wasn't house-related. I'm afraid people are going to think I've got you tied to the place, or something. Judge Owens asked after you this morning and it made me feel like I was hoarding you."

Jake smiled. It crinkled the lines around his eyes,

making them warm and inviting, and that smile was a kissable one if Mabs had ever seen one. Not that she needed to go around kissing anyone. Not that Jake wanted to be kissed. "I do get out," he promised.

"Dining out on your charm and good looks," Mabs said, "because God knows I'm not paying you."

His eyebrows rose, that kissable smile intensifying. "Do you think I'm charming and good-looking?"

Mabs made a noise that she could only describe as *inappropriate*, sort of like a 'heh' had gotten mixed up with a 'hrrr' and come out as a vocalized shorthand for *oh hell yes*! Jake's elevated eyebrows drew together in confusion. Mabs, feeling a blush coming on, squished her eyes shut, then sort of grimace-smiled at him. "You do all right, generally speaking."

"I'll take it." He returned his gaze to the walls. "So what do you think? New roof before winter?"

"Are there enough shingles? The judge wants to know if we're coming—if *you're* coming—to the Halloween thing this weekend." Mabs wrinkled her face again. She was about as smooth as a...a not-smooth thing.

"I think there are enough shingles," Jake said easily, but his eyebrows rose in amusement. "I don't know. Am I?"

"I don't know, are you? I mean, it's not dependent on me. Is it? I mean if it is you're definitely welcome to come with us, of course, that'd be great! I'd love that! Oh, but do you have a costume? Not that you need a costume. I guess grown-ups don't need costumes?" Mabs pressed her lips together, trying to stop the flow of idiotic questions.

"Who are you going as?"

"Wh-at?"

A little grin crept across Jake's mouth. "Who are you dressing as for Halloween?"

"Oh! Lady Loki."

"Loki is a lady now?"

"He is if I'm dressing as him!"

Jake's little grin became a laugh. "I guess that's fair enough. All right. Loki and Captain America, huh? I'll see what I can do. And I'll get started on the roof after the weekend, if you think I'm working too hard." His gaze flickered up again, blue eyes meeting hers, and Mabs thought she might just melt through the floor.

Except that would make a mess of all the hard work they'd done sanding the boards and relaying the runnerboards, so maybe not. "I'm sure you could use a few days off. You've been working pretty much non-stop since early September and it'll be Halloween in a couple days now."

"I've enjoyed every minute of it." He lifted his eyes, taking in the hall, then looked back down at her. "But I guess I've been in your hair, too. I hadn't thought you might want a few days in the house by yourse—"

"I don't," Mabs blurted, putting her hand on his forearm. "That wasn't what I meant at all. I just thought you might want to get out."

"I'm going to. On Saturday, with you. But I'm good, Mabs. There's not really anything in Virtue I want, so I'm fine out here, working on the house."

Man, she must be coming on like a freight train, for him to have to remind her of that again. Mabs dropped her hand, trying not to lose her smile, and said, "Great. Good. Glad to hear it. And cooking dinner, huh?"

Sudden worry creased his face. "I hope you don't mind. I like to, and I haven't gotten to cook for anybody else in ages."

"It's amazing enough to be surreal," Mabs assured him. "I just feel like I'm taking advantage of you."

The soft smile reappeared, making Mabs feel better, even if he'd put up clear *stop* signals. "I'll let you know if you are," he promised. "In the meantime, the garlic bread is probably just about done, if you want to eat."

"Oh, the garlic bread." Mabs rolled her eyes, although she hoped Jake understood she was delighted. "I suppose you made the bread from scratch, too."

"No! I bought baguettes in town and buttered and garlicked them!"

"Jake." Mabs shook her head. "I don't want to sound like a creeper, but that woman who dumped you? Was an idiot. Just so you know."

His eyebrows drew down again, an odd smile curving his mouth. "Thank you."

Mabs bumped her shoulder against his on her way into the kitchen. "Any time, big guy."

CHAPTER 10

Mabs Brannigan was gonna kill him without even trying. Without even knowing she was doing it. The way she touched his arm, the way she smiled at him, the simple sincerity with which she told him—in essence—that he was too good for the woman who'd dumped him...it was like he'd been meant to find her.

You were, his wolf said impatiently. *I keep telling you that.*

Maybe. I just don't want to go too fast. There could be things I'm not seeing.

There's a cub! There's a mate! There's a den! What else do you need to see? His wolf sent an image of a love-struck pup, mooning over a pretty wolf.

Jake had been getting a lot of that image over the past three days. It wasn't his fault he couldn't wipe the memory of Mabs's touch from his mind, or thoughts of how good it would feel to have her small soft hands in other places on his body. Or maybe it *was* his fault.

Maybe if he tried harder, he could think about other things.

But he was enjoying those thoughts so much, he didn't want to. He *liked* being around the house, cooking, working, and—it seemed—throwing together a last-minute Halloween costume so he wouldn't be shown up by Mabs and her son at the Virtue fair.

The thing was, he knew Mabs had stayed up late making both her own and Noah's costumes. Wearing something store-bought seemed cheating, in the face of that, so Jake disappeared to Sarah's house for three days, promising Mabs he'd meet them at the fair on Saturday morning.

Sarah, looking like the cat who'd stolen the cream, didn't object even once to his haranguing her for help. Carpentry, he could do; sewing machines were most of the way out of his league, since he hadn't used one since junior high home economics class. He didn't even think they *had* home ec classes anymore.

Friday evening, Sarah, looking over his handiwork, said, "You're irritatingly good at that, you know?" and Jake shrugged, pleased.

"It's like carpentry."

"It's *nothing* like carpentry."

"It is, in the sense that what matters is that if it's important to you to do a good job, you will."

"Yeah," Sarah said, somewhere between reluctant and impressed. "I guess that makes sense. I think she'll like it."

"I hope so."

Sarah gave him a sly look that he remembered from

high school, and went off without saying anything, which was infinitely worse than her making a snide comment. His wolf, baffled, said, *It is ?* and Jake groaned.

Yeah, it is.

Why?

Because if she said something I could defend myself, and instead she's just going around being smug because she thinks she's right. Jake bent his head over the costume, working on details, while his wolf asked, *Right about what?*

About her belief I'm doing this to make Mabs happy.

But you are!

That's why she's smug!

His wolf said, *I don't understand humans,* and went to sleep.

"That's okay," Jake murmured with a sigh. "I'm not sure I do either."

THE NEXT MORNING, around eleven a.m. under a crisp blue autumn sky, Jake decided it was just as well that he'd been at Sarah's house for a few days, because he thought if he'd seen Mabs in her Loki costume at her house, he might have thrown all caution to the wind and never let her go.

She wasn't tall. She would never be tall, but she'd somehow added at least three inches of height while also not looking as though her feet were bent into painfully high heels. Platform boots, he guessed, but honestly, his attention wasn't really on the boots. It was on where the boots met green leggings and rose up, fitting *every bit* as well as he'd imagined a spandex superhero suit *would* on her, to a golden belt that rode low on her hips and pointed down as if suggesting where she'd like him to direct his attention.

And it got better, because it kept fitting just as snugly through her small waist and up to her breasts, which were framed in a slightly complicated neckline, before a golden fleece of some kind fell from her shoulders, every motion revealing the long sleeves that fitted all the way to her first knuckles. She wore her purple hair loose, held away from her face by a smaller version of the golden, horned tiara that had been on the t-shirt she'd worn the first day he met her.

That, he thought, swallowing on a dry throat, was *absolutely* a goddess, and he was prepared to worship at her feet.

Noah, splendidly turned out in a miniature Cap costume, yelled, "Mr. Grooooowwwwwlllyyy!" and came running across the Virtue town square with his little shield in front of him, like he'd knock everyone and everything out of his way. It more or less worked, too, in the sense that people did dance out of the way of an adorable little superhero running full tilt toward them. Jake caught the kid and swung him into the air, laughing, then lifted him onto his shoulders. "Good to see you, Captain."

"Mom's over there!" Noah pointed imperiously, and Jake made his way toward Mabs. She met them half-way, gazing up at Jake with what he felt could accurately be described as starry eyes. "Mom!" Noah bellowed, "Look! I found Mr. Growly! He's THOR!"

"So I see." Mabs's grin was huge. "You look amazing, Jake. You put that together in three days?"

"See, I have other skills besides carpentry. And Sarah helped. A lot." Jake, grinning, put Noah down and spun like a fashion model, making a red cloak flare dramatically. The detail of his bare-armed costume had nothing on the work Mabs had put in on hers, but it was obviously enough to get the idea across, even to a four-year-old. "I'm glad you approve. You look incredible, Mabs."

"I'm not sure I can believe I'm running around in an outfit made entire of spandex," she confessed. "I don't know what I was thinking."

"Um. That, with all due respect, you have a rockin' bod and should own it?"

"Oh." Her smile slid all over the place, embarrassed and pleased and shy and delighted. "Thanks. And look at you and those *biceps*, Jake, Jesus, I shouldn't be letting you wear a shirt around the house." Horror flashed across her face. "With all due respect."

"I'd get so many splinters without one," he said apologetically, and she laughed while he considered the possibility of working without a shirt anyway. He wasn't likely to get cold, and if Mabs was inclined to enjoy that kind of thing.... "Hm?" She'd said something he hadn't quite heard.

"Why Thor?"

"Oh, well, I've seen how much trouble Cap gets into.

I thought having two gods on hand to keep an eye on him would be helpful."

Mabs laughed. "It might be almost enough. Speaking of which...." She darted off across the town square, chasing Noah, who had seen something more exciting than his mom talking to 'Mr. Growly.' Of course, to a kid his age, motes of dust dancing on the sunlight counted as more fun than adults chatting.

Jake, though, could have stood there talking to—and gazing at—Mabs all day long. All day, all week, all month, all year, all—always.

His wolf sniffed. *You should tell her that.*

I don't know if she wants to hear it. If she doesn't.... He couldn't quite let himself finish the thought. *Last time I thought I wanted to tell someone, it...didn't work.*

*Nothing will work if you **don't let it**.* His wolf bared its teeth, then snapped at the air, herding Jake after the Brannigans, as if that was commentary enough.

And maybe it was.

Every time Mabs looked at Jake through the whole afternoon, she grinned, and she looked at him a lot. More, probably, than she really should, but she liked smiling and she liked biceps and she liked short-cropped hair slicked back at the temples to pretend it was even shorter than it was, and she liked *long* legs in tight-fitting...jeans, probably, she hadn't really looked that carefully, to be honest...and she liked red cloaks and she definitely liked that whole package casually carrying her kid around on its shoulders like he belonged there.

She had, she concluded, an absolutely hopeless crush on Jake Rowly. But she guessed there were worse fates than dorking around after a gorgeous guy, so that was okay. He turned out to be surprisingly good at carnival-style games, and had won Noah a stuffed dragon four feet tall at the shoulder. He'd offered to win one for Mabs, too, but she refused, laughing, on the logic that their house was full of strange enough stuff as it was. "Next year," she said, "after the attic's cleaned out."

"It's a date," he promised, which made her feel all warm and fuzzy inside, even if she couldn't quite believe he'd be around for another year. She *had* let him buy her a cotton candy roughly the size of her torso, and kept giggling over how it disappeared with each bite. "I haven't had cotton candy since I was about Noah's age. You've got to eat some, I can't possibly eat it all. Or worse, I can, and then I'll explode out of this costume."

"You've seen that video of the cotton candy eating contest?" Jake asked, and when she shook her head, grinned broadly. "Google it, it's funny." He took some of the candy, though, and Noah took a lot of it, and by the time they got to the caramel apples Mabs thought maybe she should try one.

Jake refused, shaking his head. "I like the idea of them but then I end up with caramel in my ear and apple up my nose or something, so it's not really worth it. Old Ms. Brannigan used to make caramel apple butter, though. It was like all the promise of caramel apples with none of the disappointment."

"I have no idea what apple butter is, but that sounds amazing."

"I bet somebody around here makes it." They went around the fair, buying little jars of jams. and boxes of treats while Noah rode on what Mabs thought was the world's smallest Ferris wheel, followed by an equally small merry-go-round. He thought they were both the best, and begged to go on them again and again, even showing amazing patience for standing in line repeatedly. After the third go-around, Mabs put her foot down and got a sulky child in response, for the whole two minutes up until he discovered a hot dog stand and convinced his mommy to buy him one.

By the time he'd eaten most of it, Noah was staggering with exhaustion, and they hadn't, technically, even done any trick-or-treating. Jake murmured, "I'll carry him," and picked the little boy up easily, carting him around to the houses nearest the square, where Halloween decorations and blazing lights indicated a willingness to participate in the festivities. It only took about a block to fill the little orange plastic pumpkin they'd brought for goodies, and Noah perked up enough to eat three candy bars and an orange on the way home.

Mabs carried him up to bed and came back down without her murder tiara to find Jake making omelets in the kitchen. He glanced at her with a smile and said, "I figured some protein would be good for us after all that sugar."

"I would have gone to bed without any food. Thank you." Mabs lifted her eyebrows, smiling. "For everything. We had a wonderful day. *I* had a wonderful day."

"And Judge Owens no longer thinks you're holding me prisoner."

Mabs laughed. "Right." They'd seen the judge, and most of Virtue, in the square that afternoon. Mabs had been shyly delighted that as many people seemed to recognize and want to chat with her as much as they did with Jake, although she wasn't particularly thrilled to notice Preston Cole giving her the stink-eye from across the fair. "Want some toast?"

"If you put some of the new blackberry jam on it."

"Oooh, he drives a hard bargain." Mabs went to make toast while Jake finished the omelets and they sat at the table, silent with hunger except for when, a couple of bites in, Mabs gave an appreciative groan that made Jake smile. Even the toast seemed ridiculously good, and she pushed the plate away reluctantly when she was finished. "Where'd you come from, anyway, Jake Rowly?"

"Well..." He made a show of looking around, then pointed with his chin. "A few miles that-a-way, if you want to be particular about it. I'll show you our old house sometime. It's full of the mistakes I made learning the trade."

"Do you wish your parents hadn't sold it?"

"I don't think they would have, if any of us had imagined I'd come back to Virtue, but it's water under the bridge." He rose to do dishes, and Mabs, a little starstruck by men who did dishes, just let him, without getting up to help. It wasn't her fault the view was spectacularly good. "I thought I'd get up on the roof tomorrow and have a look around at its condition."

"Oh." Mabs straightened, suddenly feeling nervous. "I went out to the barn to look at the shingles and did some calculations. There's enough for the buttery wing roof, but not for the big one, so I was thinking we— you," she corrected herself sheepishly— "should maybe do the buttery wing, which would keep the rest of *this* part of the house warmer, 'cause there's the open door through to there, and we could do the big roof next year? After I've won the lottery or something and bought more shingles?"

"You think?" Jake rocked back on his heels, glancing toward the buttery. "All right, if that's what you want to do, I'm in."

For a moment Mabs didn't know how to respond. She trusted herself. She *did*. Mostly, she did. But when it came to making big suggestions, she realized she still expected to be mocked about it. Teased for not thinking things through, or making the wrong choices. Treated the way Noah's father had treated her, in other words. Making her doubt her own wisdom.

Jake just never, ever did that, and it wasn't until he *didn't* that she realized how tensely she'd been holding herself. How prepared she'd been to argue for her ideas, all the while starting to wonder if they'd really been good ones at all. Jake never made her feel unsure of herself.

God, she wished she'd met Jake Rowly seven years ago, instead of Brent Mitchell.

That didn't matter. Noah's father was out of her life, and had been for months now. Mabs drew a deep breath, surprised at the tremble running through her, and said, "Yeah, I think it's a good idea. I think I'll feel better with this half of the house all decently roofed."

"Okay, but I gotta warn you, Mabs. If I get started on the buttery you're going to have to bodily stop me from doing all the windows."

Mabs, standing up to dry dishes, paused at Jake's side, measuring herself against his height. "Yeah," she said dryly, "I don't think I can bodily stop you from doing anything, *Thor*."

"Wear that outfit again and I'll forget how to nail anything."

The silence following that remark was broken by both of them simultaneously collapsing to the floor, hands thrown over their faces to muffle laughter. Tears ran down Mabs's face and shone in Jake's eyes. His cheeks were a hotter red than she'd ever seen on another human being, and he had to wipe his eyes before finally managing to whisper, "That *really* didn't come out the way I meant it to."

Mabs wiped her own eyes, giggling so hard she needed to pee. "I'm just gonna...I'm gonna walk away from that, because it's either the most or the least flattering thing anybody's ever said to me and if I think about it too hard I might be mortally insulted. Oh my God. I'm just gonna, like...yeah. Oh my god."

"Me too." Jake lifted a finger like he was going to try an explanation, then shook his head. "No, I'm just gonna...I think I'll call it a night now, before I make this any worse."

"Honestly I'm not sure you can." Mabs, still giggling so hard she thought she'd better cross her legs, got up and Jake, still visibly blushing, climbed to his feet, too.

"I'm pretty sure with a little effort I could," he promised. "So...yeah, I'm going. G'night, Mabs."

"G'night, Jake." Mabs saw him out, then ran to the bathroom before she peed her costume.

～

IF SOMEONE HAD TOLD her a year earlier that she would come home every night to a visibly improving house and a gorgeous man she had a side-splittingly funny in-jokes type relationship with, Mabs simply wouldn't have believed them. A few weeks after Halloween, though, it was true every day, and she couldn't remember ever being happier.

In late November, she came home to a functional living room behind the kitchen, and finished windows. Overwhelmed, she actually sat down to cry. Jake had leaned so hard on social credit to get it done, and it worried her, but he'd seemed so *sure* that it was the right thing to do, that Mabs had gradually let herself be talked into it. Coming home to the last of the old, wobbly glass panes framed up as the atmospheric outer pane of new, triple-paned windows was simply over-whelming.

Both Noah and Wolf had climbed all over her, trying to reassure her with hugs and kisses. A long cuddle helped her regain her equilibrium, and then, pink-cheeked with heat, she turned the kitchen ther-mostat down even though it was November, proving that Jake had been right about it being worth the social credit spend. She would be paying off the loans until the end of time, but the house was cozy, her kid was wonderful, and it didn't suck to have an incredibly gorgeous man around the house to crush on, even if he wasn't interested in relationships. Unrequited lust gave Mabs a direction to expend some of that kind of energy in without actually having to worry about getting involved with somebody.

And Jake Rowly was a *great* subject for unrequited lust. He cooked dinner regularly, for heaven's sake, and usually left it covered on the table with an apologetic note for having been in her kitchen. He took things down off the high kitchen shelves for her, when they were both in there together, and smiled at her good-natured grumbling about tall people designing kitchens.

They'd come to a kind of unspoken arrangement that the downstairs bathroom was mostly his to come in from the barn to use. Mabs *might* have learned to time her morning wake-up routine in such a way as to occasionally glimpse him jogging back out of the house post-shower, sometimes shirtless.

She'd never appreciated how amazing a well-developed back could be, before that. The first time she'd done that—accidentally!—she'd spent the whole day so mesmerized by the memory of rivulets of water sliding down his spine that she'd messed up half a dozen orders at the diner, which never, ever happened. Luckily, no one had been too upset, but boy, it was like she needed a brain scrubber to stop the fantasies of tracing those droplets with her tongue, or turning him around to follow the lines of water elsewhere on his body, or maybe just somehow accidentally getting in the shower with him and—

Fortunately—or not—most of the time she was too *tired* to indulge in many fantasies, although it got easier as the weeks went by and they spent several evenings working on something quiet in the house. The buttery roof took shape while she was at the diner during the day, with Jake texting pictures every couple of hours when he felt he'd done something worth admiring.

Everybody at the diner wanted to see the pictures, and Sarah demanded to see them every afternoon when she picked Noah up from the library. *Especially*, Sarah emphasized, the selfie pics, which occasionally featured Jake without a shirt on, if it was warm enough that afternoon. Most of Mabs's conversations with Sarah on that topic went "shut up shut up shut up shut *up*," until Noah scolded her for saying mean words to her friend. She apologized, both to Sarah and Noah, and Noah invited Sarah over to Thanksgiving as proof that Mabs really meant it.

"I'd love to," Sarah said cautiously, eyeing Mabs to make sure it was actually all right.

"We're not having a huge party," Mabs warned. "I just want to do something for our first Thanksgiving in the house. It would be wonderful if you were part of it."

"I make a mean green bean casserole," Sarah promised. "Just tell me when."

"Well. Next Thursday."

"Okay, tell me what time!"

Mabs laughed. "About two, I think."

"I'll see you there." Sarah waved goodbye, and Mabs scooped Noah up to bring him home.

SHE WAS STILL WRANGLING Noah out of the car at home when her phone rang. Noah grabbed for it, yelling, "I want to say hi!" and she nearly dropped both him and the phone trying to deal with them at the same time. Jake, who'd been up on the roof as she drove up, came down just in time to grab Noah and set him on his feet, allowing Mabs to answer the phone just before it stopped ringing.

"Hi, hello, this is Mabs?" She mouthed 'thank you' at Jake, who smiled, winked, and chased Noah around the front yard to keep him from participating in Mabs's phone conversation.

"Hi, Mabs? This is Erica down at Heartfire Massage. You'd said you were interested in becoming a therapist, but our classes were all booked out?"

Mabs's heart knocked so hard she had to lean against the car. "Yeah?"

"Well, someone just dropped out of the course starting this afternoon. I don't suppose you can take their place?"

Mabs said, "Oh my God," so softly that Jake looked up from chasing Noah with a worried expression. Mabs, lower lip in her teeth, stared at him as she shook her head. "I don't...I don't think I can, Erica. I don't have..."

She didn't have someone to watch Noah. Except Jake Rowly was standing right there, and the truth was, Mabs and her silly crush trusted the man with her life. More importantly, she trusted him with Noah's life. She croaked, "Hang on," into the phone, and held it against her chest, cheeks flushed as she looked at Jake. "Could I...ask a huge favor, Jake?"

"Are you okay?" He stepped closer to her, big hands

extended like he would support her if she needed it. "You look upset."

"No, I..." Mabs took a deep breath, trying to steady herself. "I've always wanted to be a massage therapist, see, and an opening in a class has just come up, but it's right now, I'd have to go to town *now*, and—"

"I'd love to watch Noah, if you're okay with that."

Mabs threw herself into Jake's arms, hugging him. Literally threw, like, she accidentally threw her phone on the ground, but he caught her and picked her up with such strength and warmth she just didn't care. God, he smelled so good, and was so tall and strong, and his body felt so good against hers, and she could just wrap her legs around his hips and—

—and he put her down, smiling, and said, "Better get your phone."

"Right. Right!" Right. There was no one in Virtue that he wanted to have a relationship with. Which was *fine*, because Mabs had too much to do anyway. Like snatch her phone up, exhale relief that the screen hadn't broken, and put it to her ear to say, "Erica? I can make it."

"Oh, thank goodness! I thought the house had fallen on you or something. Great. Can you be here at four?"

"Yes!" Mabs did a dance as she hung up, then turned to find Jake watching her with the softest smile imaginable.

"I didn't know you wanted to be a massage therapist."

"Yeah, it's, I—" Mabs's excitement suddenly fell away into uncertainty. She put her hands over her face, trying to slow her breathing. "I always wanted to," she whispered into her palms. "I never told—I hardly ever told anybody it was my dream, and the last person I did tell..." She pressed her lips together and shook her head.

Jake waited a moment, then, gently, said, "Mabs?"

"Nothing, um. It's just...it was Noah's dad, and he...he really kind of made fun of me. More than that. He made me feel stupid for thinking I could do something like that. I'm short, you know? I can't haul people around, really, or...I don't know. Maybe it's *not* a good idea."

"Mabs." Jake reached for one of her hands, not making contact until she actually put her hand in his. "Mabs, it's not stupid. It's amazing that you have the chance to follow a dream. I'm pretty sure massage is a case where size really doesn't matter. You don't have to be a giant to understand how muscles work, or how to release tension points. I think it's an incredible idea. You should go for it."

Mabs looked at their entwined hands, felt the warmth and certainty not just of Jake's touch, and met his eyes to whisper, "Thank you. Thanks, Jake, I...I don't think anybody's ever really encouraged me before. And with this, it's not easy getting a steady enough babysitter to do something like regular classes, so I kind of just...wrote it off." Her smile came back, slowly, although her heart ached with a little uncertainty, still. "So thank you for this. And the encouragement. I promise I'll find somebody to watch him when I've got the class schedule. Sarah will know somebody...."

"Mabs, I'm here, I'm around, if you don't mind...he's a great kid. I don't mind watching him."

"Oh my God, Jake." Mabs had never experienced her heart melting before. Not with an adult, anyway. Noah made her heart melt a lot, but it was different when a tall, handsome, hard-bodied, insanely competent, kind, smart, funny guy just...stepped up. "Jake, you've already done so much for me already. I mean, you've been cooking dinner, for heaven's sake. And you're really *good* at it," she added helplessly.

Jake grinned. "I cooked today, too. Go eat. You've got a class to get to. We'll figure out the regular minding for Noah this evening, all right? I've got him, this afternoon." His eyebrows lifted. "I probably won't get much work done around the house."

Mabs, feeling much better and starting to smile again, also rolled her eyes. "I *guess* I'll forgive you, although, jeez, if you can't watch a cyclone disguised as a four-year-old and his pet whirlwind the four-month-old puppy *and* renovate an entire house in an afternoon, what good are you?"

"I have it on some authority I'm pretty good," he informed her loftily, and Mabs, opening the front door, managed to walk right into the frame.

Bouncing off, rubbing her shoulder, she croaked, "I'll have to take your word for it," and fled toward food and all the thoughts of just *what* Jake Rowly might be authoritatively good at.

CHAPTER 12

Mabs had flung herself into his arms, and Jake had wanted to never, ever let her go. He'd had to, of course, but he thought the memory of her soft warm body in his arms might stay with him forever. All he'd wanted to do was bury his face in her hair and hold on. At least, for that moment, that's what he'd wanted, because simply carrying her upstairs to a bedroom would have needed to wait until after Noah was asleep.

Holding her, Jake thought, would have been enough.

You brought food, his wolf said with a sniff that was meant to be encouraging. *Females appreciate good hunters. And you'll watch the cubs. Females like that too. The den is improving. When will you tell her about me?*

Jake chuckled softly. *When the time is right.*

The wolf groaned. *She's your mate. The time is never wrong.*

"And yet," Jake murmured aloud. He went out to the

porch, calling, "Your mom's eating, Noah. Do you want to eat with her?"

"MY MOM'S EATING *NOAH* ?" Noah shrieked with laughter and fell over, kicking his feet and pounding his fists on the ground. Wolf ran circles around and over him, licking his face and wagging his tail so hard it blurred. After a minute of theatrical hysterics, Noah jumped up and ran past Jake into the house, yelling, "Mama! Mama! Mr. Growly says you're eating Noah! Don't eat me! I'm all chewy!"

"Oh, I bet you'd be tender and delicious," Mabs said from the kitchen. What sounded like a train wreck ensued, Mabs roaring like a monster while Noah screamed happily. "Gotcha! Nom nom nom!"

"No, Mama, no! Don't eat me! Don't eeeeeaaaaaat meeeeee!" Noah collapsed in a pile of giggles as Jake, smiling, came into the kitchen. "Mr. Growly you're RIGHT Mama WAS eating me! Help! Help!"

Jake waggled his fingers threateningly at Mabs, who laughed. "No, you can't tickle me right now, I have to finish eating and go into town. Noah, honey, Mr. Rowly is going to watch you for a couple of hours, okay? I have to go do something."

Noah, sitting at the table, said, "Okay," with the casual air of a child who felt completely safe, and Jake, who didn't really think of himself as a Grinch, felt his heart grow three sizes anyway. The Brannigan family was well and truly under his skin, and the truth was, Jake Rowly didn't want it any other way.

Noah was still eating when Mabs gave him a kiss, mouthed *thank you* again at Jake, gratefully, and went running off to her class. Well, driving off: running to town would take too long. The minute she was out the door, Noah gave Jake a sly look. "Can I watch some television, Mr. Growly?"

Jake laughed. "No."

The little boy stuck his lip out in a pout, but obviously hadn't expected any other answer. He finished up his dinner—or maybe it was second lunch, because at only 3:30 in the afternoon, Jake was certain Noah would want more food later—and ran outside with Wolf bouncing along behind him.

Mabs let him run around outside without immediate supervision all the time, but she'd never left *Jake* in charge before. His heart absolutely rattled at the thought of anything happening to Noah on his watch, so he followed him out and sat on the porch to keep an eye out. The boy and puppy raced all over the place, involved in some complicated game that Jake, a mere adult, couldn't be expected to understand the intricacies of.

Nothing had ever felt so right.

After at least half an hour of exhaustive play, Noah came staggering up to the porch, gasping, "Can I have some water, Mr. Growly?" and Jake, grinning, got up to get the kid a glass of water.

"Why do you call me Mr. 'Growly,' anyway, Noah?"

"Your voice is nice and growly," Noah caroled after him. "Can Wolf have water too?"

"Wolf has a water bowl!"

"He likes water best from a GLASS!"

So do I, Jake's wolf announced, and with the argument coming from two sides, Jake, grinning, got a second glass of water for the puppy. His wolf perked its ears at the sound of a car in the drive, much too early for Mabs to be back. Jake glanced out the kitchen window and went still as a good-looking dark blonde guy got out of his car and leaned on the front gate.

"Hey, kid! Noah! Hey, Noah, it's your daddy! Do you remember me, buddy? Wow, you're so big! Is your mom home?" In a lower voice, not meant to be heard, the man muttered, "Oh great, a dog."

Noah, who'd been running full tilt toward the gate to greet the visitor, stopped dead halfway down the path. Wolf skidded a few feet past him, then circled back to stand at Noah's calf, his whole furry body trembling with tension. Even from the kitchen, even in human form, Jake could smell Noah's confusion and nervousness.

He didn't really think about it. He put the water glasses down carefully on the counter, wiped his hands on his jeans, and walked out of the house to stand with Noah.

Not as a man, though. He shifted as soon as he'd turned the door handle, nosing the door open and trotting down the porch steps to put himself firmly in front of the little boy and his protective puppy. He couldn't say why, except the primal force of his animal shape felt right. It even felt less aggressive, in its way. Noah's father might pick a fight with a man, try to establish some kind of unearned territory markers, but unless he was toting a gun, he wasn't likely to mess with a wolf.

And he didn't seem to have a gun. He said, "Holy *fuck* !" and backed up from the gate. "Jesus, Noah, get away from there, that's a fucking wolf."

Noah patted Jake's spine and bent to pick up Wolf under his front legs, showing the puppy's fat tummy to the world. "*This* is Wolf, and that's an inappropriate word to use around children."

Jake's jaw dropped open in a wolfy laugh, his tongue lolling. It took everything he had to keep his tail from wagging at the little boy's scolding tone, and his laugh turned into a yawn that—totally coincidentally—showed off *all* his long ivory teeth.

Noah's father's voice rose. "No, kid, *that's* a fucking *wolf* ! Get out of there! Get—Jesus, what the fuck is your mother thinking? You have to come with me right now, Noah."

Noah stepped forward to put his hand on Jake's spine again. "This is Mr. Growly," he said as astonishment shot through Jake, "and I don't know *you*. Mama says not to go with strangers."

"I'm your goddamn father, kid!"

Jake growled, low and deep in his throat. Noah's father went white and backed up until he hit the side of his car, then scrambled into it with a yelled, "I'm coming back for you, Noah!"

He sped off in a cloud of dust and Noah tightened his fingers in Jake's fur, whispering, "I didn't like him, Mr. Growly."

Jake shifted back into his human form and caught

the little boy and his puppy in his arms, hugging them hard. "Neither did I, Noah. Neither did I."

Noah hung on for a minute, then squirmed loose, his eyes enormous. "Mr. Growly, how did you do that? Can I do that? Can WOLF do that? Where did your clothes go? How come you didn't bite that mean man? Can I see your teeth? Sometimes Wolf makes me sneeze. Do you make yourself sneeze? Is he going to come back? Will you bite him if he does? Can I have a cookie?"

Jake reeled under the barrage of questions, ending on a laugh. "I was born able to do this, so no, I'm afraid you and Wolf can't do it. My clothes are kind of like my fur, so they stay with me when I change. I hardly ever make myself sneeze, it's not nice to bite people, and," he said, standing to offer Noah a hand, "yes, you may have a cookie. How did you know it was me?"

Noah had to put Wolf down in order to take Jake's hand, and looked up at him nonplussed. "You were the only other person here. Can I have TWO cookies?"

"I was the only other p..." Jake trailed off, then shook his head, smiling. "I guess that makes sense. And yes, you may have two cookies."

Noah, with the air of a child who thought he might be on to a good thing, said, "May I have THREE cookies?"

Jake burst out laughing. "No. Two cookies and some milk."

"Okay, Mr. Growly!" Noah let go of his hand and ran into the house, Wolf bouncing at his heels. Jake gazed after them in amazement, hardly knowing what to think. He was going to owe Mabs one hell of an explanation, but Noah had just accepted the impossible with hardly more than a blink.

See? his wolf asked, smug. *Easy.*

MABS GOT HOME in the middle of dinner, glowing with happiness. Jake didn't try to stop Noah from rushing straight to her with shouts of everything that had transpired in her absence. His narrative about a mean man and Mr. Growly being a BIG DOG was a little jumbled, and some of Mabs's glow had faded by the time she got Noah back to the table and asked Jake, with a quirk of worried eyebrows, what had happened.

"Someone who said he was Noah's father came by," Jake said quietly. "Good-looking blonde guy, mid-thirties? He didn't give his name."

"Brent? I just can't—I've barely even seen him since Noah was born." Mabs sounded more baffled than angry or upset. "I don't know how he'd even find us. What did he want?"

"I don't know. I kind of ran him off before there was much conversation."

To his surprise, Mabs flashed a smile. "You're good at that, aren't you? Thanks. What...on earth was Noah talking about? A big dog? Did Wolf suddenly turn into Cerberus or something?"

Now! his wolf said. *Tell her now!*

Jake, though, couldn't help smiling at the idea of the puppy turning into a three-headed hellhound. "Not exactly. Can I explain that after Noah's gone to bed? It might take a while."

His wolf said *hnf*, but Mabs, who had no reason to expect sudden shapeshifters in her life, said, "Okay, sure," easily, then squeezed his arm. "Thank you, Jake. I know it's not your job to end up standing between me and annoying men who show up on my property, but you're really good at it and I appreciate it."

"I'll be glad to do it as long as you need me."

"Watch it," Mabs said lightly. "I might need you for a long time."

CHAPTER 13

*H*er first massage therapy class had been such a rush Mabs hadn't thought anything could bring her down from it. But if anything could, it would be the baffling reappearance of Noah's father. In fact, if anything *should*, it was Brent's return.

Somehow, though, it wasn't rattling her nearly as badly as it should. Not with Jake nearby, providing a kind of safety net that she hadn't even realized she wanted.

It was going to suck, Mabs realized, when Jake Rowly moved on. She'd come to rely on him over the past couple of months, and not just in an *oh God he's so pretty* way, although she could rarely look at the man without him taking her breath away. His presence around the house comforted her, and the care he'd taken in making her home warm and secure went far beyond what she could ever repay him for.

And dealing with Brent, or Preston Cole, for that

matter, would be harder without Jake around, but that was something Mabs was going to have to get used to. She tucked Noah into bed, listened in amusement to his repetition of the story about the mean man and Mr. Growly, who was Mr. Growly *and*, apparently, a Big Dog, and left him to sleep with his puppy sprawled at the foot of his bed.

"If I've got this right," she murmured, still amused as she came into the kitchen to find Jake at the table, "Brent showed up while Noah and Wolf were playing in the yard, then a big dog came out of the house, growled at Brent to scare him off, and then turned into you and you all came into the house for milk and cookies?"

Jake rubbed a fingertip over his eyebrow, as if trying to find an itch that he could hide behind. "Well. Wolf didn't have cookies. Chocolate's bad for dogs. The rest of it, though...he got that pretty much right."

"Jake." Mabs ducked head to give him what would be a look over the top edge of her glasses, if she wore glasses. "Don't be ridiculous. I'm sure everything was okay with Brent, if you were here, so why don't you tell me what really happened?"

He stood and ran a hand through his hair, a nervous gesture that made the greying strands stand up every which way. Mabs's eyebrows drew down. *Nervous* was not a word she associated with Jake Rowly. Handsome, kind, competent, generous, talented—there were lots of words she *could* associate with him, but nervous definitely wasn't one. "Jake?"

"What if he did get it right, Mabs? What if Noah

told you exactly what had happened, and he was right about all of it?"

"Jake..." A knot of discomfort tied itself in Mabs's stomach. "Jake, did something actually awful happen? What happened? You're scaring me."

"Nothing awful happened." His voice was very soft as he walked to the other end of the kitchen, putting the whole length of the room between them. "Noah explained it all already. It's just that what he explained is impossible to believe, unless you see it."

"Jake, I don't understand, what are you talking abo—"

Jake Rowly, at the far end of the kitchen, faced her, spread his hands in a shrug, and turned into a wolf.

MABS SHRIEKED in the back of her throat, hands clamped over her mouth so the only sound that emerged was a kind of strangled gurgle. Her knees cut out and she sat hard into a kitchen chair. Jake lay down flat on his belly, head extended between his paws and the very tip of his tail wagging.

Exactly like Wolf when the puppy was afraid he might be in trouble.

A slightly hysterical giggle escaped from behind Mabs's hands in the same way the shriek had. Jake's ears perked and his eyes—big blue eyes, although Mabs didn't think wolves came by blue eyes naturally—but then, why would a shapeshifting man-wolf come by anything naturally? *Anyway,* his eyes widened hopefully, and Mabs blurted another giggle.

Jake's tail started wagging harder and he crept forward a few inches, belly still flat on the floor. Mabs giggled again and he squirmed forward faster, getting his feet under him enough to scootch across the floor with his belly about two inches off it. She sat there, still giggling, until he crawled all the way down the kitchen to her and put his chin on her foot, eyes rolled hopefully up to see her expression.

Mabs, being not made of stone, bent and rubbed his ears. Jake pushed his head into her hand, whining. She slid out of the chair, and he sat up into a furry hug and licked her ear. Mabs whispered, "Jake?" and he shifted in her arms, catching her when the change in his shape unbalanced her.

He whispered, "Sorry," but all she could think of was his strength, the ease with which he'd caught her, and the warmth of his arms around her. He was so *close.* Mabs hadn't been close enough to kiss someone in longer than she liked to think, and she'd nearly lifted her mouth to his before she remembered Jake Rowly was in Virtue to avoid relationships, not find one.

She pulled back, heart hammering, and pushed her hands through her hair, wetting her lips before croaking, "Um...how... Where...do your clothes go..."

Did she imagine it, or was there a flash of disappointment in his blue eyes as she pulled away? She probably imagined it, from the ease with which he rolled back a little, and chuckled. "Noah asked that too. They shift with me, like they're my fur." A grin danced across his face. "And no, that doesn't mean if I shift while naked, I'm a furless wolf."

"I wasn't going to ask!" protested Mabs, who had totally been going to ask. Then she put her hands over her mouth and edged a little farther back, trying to see all of Jake at once, as if she'd be able to see the wolf, too, if she looked hard enough. "Jake...how..."

"Runs in the family," he said softly, as if afraid he would chase her away. "Back in the day there were a lot of shifters in Virtue, Mom says. People running from persecution in the old world, I guess. I didn't know any others growing up, though, so I guess it's run its course, maybe."

Mabs kind of heard all of that, and sort of got that it didn't mean what popped into her mind next. She still squeaked, "Are you a *werewolf*?"

Jake's gorgeous grin flashed again. "Nah. Were-wolves—well, okay, first, I've never met one, so I don't know for sure, but if the stories about them are at all real, then they're tied to the phases of the moon and I'm not. I'm a shapeshifter, so I can just change when-ever I want."

Mabs flapped both hands in expectation and Jake shifted, his grin still fixed firmly in place on a wolfy face. He had very large teeth.

And Mabs bet they'd scared the ever-loving shit out of Brent. She suddenly found a huge grin on her own face. "Okay. Okay, I get it. Not a werewolf. So you don't, uh, bite people and change them?"

Jake, shifting back, said, "Well, I've never tried, but no, it's genetic, not contagious. And if I'm laying it all on the line..." His expression went serious and Mabs's heart nearly stopped with hope. Maybe he'd only said there was nobody to have a relationship with in Virtue because he hadn't really known her then. Maybe he wanted as much to stay as she wanted him to. Maybe—?

"I guess I *could* be a werewolf," Jake said solemnly. "Stories about shapeshifters do tend to get...embellished in the re-telling." His eyes sparkled, and Mabs heard herself give a weak little laugh in response.

"Sure," she said faintly. "Right. Of course they do. Because..." She couldn't think of anything else to say, and just sat there looking at him for what felt like forever.

He looked like the same guy he'd been all along. Tall, ruggedly handsome, kind-hearted. Reliable. Competent. Insanely, insanely attractive. Maybe a hint of shyness or hope in his blue eyes, now. Or wariness, maybe, as if he wasn't sure whether she'd throw him out. "It must be hard," she whispered.

Surprise drew his eyebrows down, and she spread her hands a little. "I mean, you must not tell very many people, right? It must be hard to have to go around your whole life keeping such a big part of yourself from the people aro...oh." Her voice softened as sympathy struck her. "Is that what happened with the one who got away? She couldn't handle it?"

"I never told her." The words came in a rush and Jake looked away, making a face of embarrassment. "The time never seemed right."

And that, Mabs thought, had been with The One, or

at least, with the person he'd thought had been the one. She couldn't imagine that he'd have ever told *her*, unless he'd been forced to, in a situation like this. Heart aching, she reached out and took one of his hands. "Thank you. Thank you for risking your secret to keep Noah safe, Jake. I won't tell anyone."

"No, I guess I didn't think you would." His eyebrows stayed drawn, more confusion than surprise now. "You're not freaked out?"

"I mean, I'm a little freaked out." Mabs laughed, put her face in her hands, then lifted her gaze again to meet Jake's. "You were here to protect my kid, Jake. I know you would have done the same thing whether you were a—" she nearly spluttered the words—"a *shapeshifter* or not, but...you didn't have to let anybody, much less me and Noah, know that. You could have just been your-self, your...human self...and done the same thing, but you thought this was the better way, didn't you?"

At his nod, she spread her hands again. "I guess I'd be kind of a jerk to completely flip out over you deciding that revealing what's got to be the biggest secret in your life is the best way to keep my son safe. I am absolutely *dying* to know everything in the whole world about shapeshifters now, because oh my God, who knew there were shapeshifters?! But...I guess if I'm freaked out it's because oh my God, who knew there were shapeshifters? It's not because you're one."

Tension she hadn't even known was in him drained out of Jake until she thought he might lie back down on the floor like his wolf self had done. Mabs reached out to pat his shoulder just as he looked up, and somehow ended up sliding her fingers right along his temple into his short greying hair.

Jake's breath caught and he lifted his hand, capturing hers against his head. His fingers curled at her wrist, warm and strong, and his breath trickled over the soft skin there, like the promise of a kiss. His gaze held that promise, too, or at least a question of it, and Mabs was wetting her lips, ready to answer, when Noah wailed, "Mommy?" from upstairs. "Mommy, I had a bad dream!"

Mabs closed her eyes in a whole-body grimace, and, with sweet, gentle thoughts of murder on her mind, went to check on her kid.

CHAPTER 14

Jake sat back with a thump when Mabs left him, nearly clobbering his head on the underside of the kitchen table. Nobody who ever wanted to have sex again, he thought, should have kids.

Not that he expected telling a beautiful woman that he was a shapeshifter should definitely lead to sex, but it had looked promising there for a moment. The idea of gathering Mabs in his arms, of kissing her and murmuring her name into that gorgeous purple hair, of picking her up, carrying her to bed, of simply *being* with her, was...really appealing.

Of course it is, his wolf said impatiently. *She's your mate and you've been avoiding her for moons and moons!*

*I haven't been **avoiding** her! I've been hanging out with her all along! And she has a kid! And an ex! You don't just swoop in and say 'Hi, I'm your fated mate' to a woman in that position!*

The wolf sniffed. *Scaredy-cat.*

Jake sent back an image of a teenage afternoon when he'd been sneaking around the woods in wolf form and somebody's house cat had taken umbrage at his presence on its territory. The cat, which couldn't have weighed more than twelve pounds, fluffed up, bounced across the thin forest floor at him, hissing, snarling and batting at him the whole way. Jake's feet had gotten so tangled up trying to run away that he'd fallen down a hill and into the same stream that ran by Mabs's place.

Wet, like clothes, remained, when a shifter changed shapes.

*That was **different**,* his wolf said with affronted dignity.

"Mmm," Jake said aloud. "Cats aren't scaredy, and neither am I."

Mabs came down the stairs again as he spoke, looking much more worn-out than she had when she'd gone up. "Are you down here talking to yourself?" Her voice, soft so as to not wake Noah again, was also gently teasing, as was her smile.

"Not exactly." Jake finally got off the floor, stretching idly. "My wolf is...it's like an inner voice, only more of a smartass. At least, I hope other people's inner voices aren't that snarky."

Mabs leaned in the kitchen door, smiling. "What was—he? It? They?—snarking about?"

"He thought I should have told you a while ago and was smug that you took it well."

Her eyebrows rose. "Well, to be fair to, uh, human-you, I don't know if I would have six weeks ago. Tell him to be nice to you or I won't scratch the top of his head again."

Hey!

Jake laughed. "He objects. I don't know if it'll make him stop giving me a hard time, but it was a good threat."

Mabs wriggled her shoulders, a visible sign of satisfaction that also wriggled the rest of her in an incredibly distracting, attractive way. She'd taken off her bra while upstairs, leaving her breasts free to jiggle under the snug fit of her t-shirt, and that jiggle went all the way down, shaking her little soft belly, her hips, her...Jake got kind of caught around her hips, really, forgetting to draw his gaze any farther down, or any farther up again, for that matter.

"I was wondering," she said, apparently not noticing he'd fixated on her hips, "I was wo—well—it's—no—never mind."

That was enough to bring his attention back from the study of her hips, although he quite intensely wanted to resume that as soon as possible. "Never mind what?"

She opened a hand and closed it again, then repeated that, lifting it like she might conduct her speech before losing her nerve again. "Um. No, it's...no. I don't think...so."

"Mabs." Curious, amused, a little worried, Jake crossed to her, trying to get close enough to share secrets without looming. It was hard not to loom; she was eight inches shorter than Jake. He had to fight the urge to turn into a wolf, which at least wouldn't loom, but which was a great deal harder to hold a conversation with. Instead he put his hands out, palms up, from a few feet away, inviting whatever she had to say. "What is it?"

"It's just that—I don't know how he found us. My parents and friends sure wouldn't have told him where I'd gone. I guess somebody at work could have, but I really just said I was moving upstate, not even where to. Honestly, I can't even imagine him bothering." Mabs went around Jake, all the way into the kitchen, and got a drink of water, giving the faucets a suspicious, cautious look as she did. They both did that, partly out of not trusting the faucet but mostly to make the other one laugh. Now, even with her dancing around whatever she wanted to say, it still made Jake smile.

The smile seemed to reassure her. She went to sit at the table, putting her water glass down and spinning it in its own ring of condensation. "I wasn't exactly running away from him, you know? But I wasn't *not*, either. Wasn't-not, like...I'm not on social media and changed my phone number and provider when I got up here, not. And my email address."

A kernel of anger flared deep in Jake's chest. He took a careful breath, trying not to let it blaze out of control as he asked, carefully, "Did he hurt you?"

She glanced up, then back down at her glass, but shook her head no. "No, not physically. Not even verbally, exactly. He was...gas-lighty. I kind of got to where I just...I thought I couldn't do stuff without him. Like I wasn't good enough at things." She swirled the water in her glass, lips compressed. "Except I guess he wasn't the totally controlling kind of gas-lighter, just...a jerk, I guess, because he was furious when I got pregnant, though, like I'd planned it to get at his vast fortune." She looked up again, a spark of humor in her eyes and in the twist of her mouth as she dropped her voice into a movie trailer narrator's tone. "Spoiler: he did not have a vast fortune.

"Anyway," she said in her regular voice, "we split up. So obviously he wasn't into totally controlling me, because he didn't want anything to do with me or Noah. Which was *fine*, I didn't want anything to do with him, either, but then he kept coming around, once every six or eight months, I guess. Just often enough to make me uncomfortable, you know? So I couldn't quite move on. He didn't even want to actually see Noah or anything. He just wanted to make me twitchy."

We should have bitten him, Jake's wolf said, and Jake couldn't really find fault with the statement.

"Even before I inherited the house I'd filed for termination of his parental rights since he's literally never met Noah, but you know how those things are." She glanced up again, saw from Jake's expression that he didn't, and half smiled. "Difficult," she supplied. "It's hard, even if it's a clear case of abandonment. Judges don't like ruling against biological parents. Anyway, the point of all this is I...I don't really think he's dangerous, but would you...I'd..." She exhaled, muttered, "Jeez," and looked up to meet his eyes with determination.

"I know I'm asking a lot, but would you maybe mind staying in the house until I get rid of him?"

She kept talking—"It's ridiculous, asking somebody

if they'd rather sleep in a house than a barn, but I don't even have an extra bed in the house right now, the parlor side just isn't sleep-in-able yet, and I know it's weird because I know all you want to do is help out building around here and I still haven't even been able to pay you hardly anything and—?"

All Jake heard, though, was that Mabs needed him. All he knew was that the very idea filled him with joy. It didn't even matter *why* she needed him, although he and his wolf were in full agreement that the opportunity to bite her ex couldn't be passed up. She needed him. Him. Jake Rowly.

No one had needed him in a long, long time.

She was obviously embarrassed by the very idea, though, and had just about talked herself out of it before Jake said, "I'd be glad to!"

"What?" Her voice went faint. "Really?"

"Really. What are friends for?"

His wolf, hopelessly, said, *Friends?*, and, with the sense of giving up, took a nap.

Mabs's gaze flickered to her water glass and back. "Running ex-boyfriends and pushy realtors off?"

"Without a doubt." Jake smiled and Mabs's shoulders dropped visibly.

"Thanks. I guess...tomorrow? I can get a bed of some kind for the dining room? Would that be okay?"

"Mabs, if you want, I can sleep in here tonight." Jake didn't want to sound too eager, but he didn't want her to keep herself awake with worry all night, either. "I—"

"But the couch in the living room isn't long enough

for you..." Mabs sounded unhappy, but he couldn't help the increasing size of his...smile.

"I'm a wolf, Mabs. I can curl up in front of your door, or even on the porch, if you want. I'm not going to get cold or uncomfortable."

Mabs opened her mouth and closed it again, nonplussed. "I can't ask you to do that."

"You're not," Jake pointed out, genuinely cheerful. "I volunteered. Honestly, give me a fluffy rug and I'm great."

"A flu...Are you out there sleeping in the barn as a wolf?" Mabs cracked up suddenly, giggles overwhelming whatever worries she had. "Have I been one early morning away from discovering my carpenter is a... *timber wolf*?"

Jake started protesting, "No, no," to her first question before the second was finished, and was caught off-guard by a guffaw that made Mabs leap forward and clap a hand over his mouth. Jake looked guiltily toward the stairs, but Noah didn't complain, and Mabs sat back down again, steadying the water glass she'd nearly knocked over.

Then they were both suddenly laughing again, tears of amusement sparkling in Mabs's eyes. "Timber wolf," she said in a whisper this time. "I'm pretty funny."

"You are." Jake's grin was so broad it hurt. "I never thought of me that way before, but yeah, I guess I am. I'll stay," he promised. "I'll sleep at the front door. Mabs?"

"Yeah?" She met his eyes, and Jake had to remind himself for the hundredth time that she hadn't hired him for anything other than house repairs. Not that he'd want to have been *hired* for most of the other things he had in mind, but...that wasn't the point.

The point was, "I'm glad you asked. I'm glad I can help you out."

"I'm glad you told me your secret." Mabs wrinkled her nose, which was so cute it brought Jake all the way back around to feeling like catching her in his arms and kissing her really would be an awfully good idea. "I would have asked you to stay in the house anyway, but having a giant wolf-man i—"

"I'm not a wolf-man!" Jake did his best Lon-Cheney-as-Wolf-Man pose and Mabs shook with laughter again. "Shapeshifter," he told her, grinning. "I'm a shapeshifter. Big difference."

"Okay, shapeshifter. I can see I'm going to have to learn a whole new vocabulary here. So having a giant wolf shapeshifter in the house is even more...protecty...than having just a big tall strong handsome man around, so...thank you."

"Oh, so I'm handsome now?" Jake couldn't have been happier at the confession if he'd tried. *She thinks I'm handsome!*

His wolf rolled its eyes and otherwise ignored him as Mabs wrinkled her nose again and said, "I guess you'll do, yeah," as she rose from the table. "Look, Jake, we probably have a million things to talk about regarding the house and Brent and, I don't know, *shapeshifters*, but I'm bushed. I'm gonna go to bed. Are you sure about this?"

Rather than answer with words, Jake shifted into

his wolf form as he stood, and went to lean heavily against Mabs's hip. She hesitated, then curled her fingers in his ruff before kneeling to wrap her arms around his shoulders and bury her face in his fur. He heard her muffled, "Thank you," in his bones, and trotted to the bottom of the stairs behind her, then curled up at their foot, his nose pointed attentively toward the front door.

The memory of that hug kept him warm all night.

CHAPTER 15

Jake was human again by the time Mabs came downstairs, Noah in tow, the next morning. He waved them off and Mabs, getting Noah into his car seat on the almost-frosty morning, wondered at her ability to adapt to her carpenter being a shapeshifting wolf as if it was nothing particularly unusual. Somehow, though, it seemed perfectly in keeping with Jake's slightly solitary nature, and she suddenly wondered if Sarah knew. She'd called him a lone wolf, but then, that was just a thing people *said*. It didn't mean anything.

Unless it did.

"Hey, Noah?" Her son was involved in a library book, and made a vaguely interested noise response. "Probably we shouldn't tell anybody about Mr. Rowly turning into a big dog, okay?"

"Okay, Mommy." He turned the page, and Mabs couldn't help chuckling. Maybe taking shapeshifters in stride was a family trait. There were probably worse traits to have.

Like Brent Mitchell's decision to hunt them down. Mabs made a face at the road and put that thought out of her mind for the moment, since there wasn't anything she could really do about it, and Jake was home keeping the house safe.

She dropped Noah off at the library, muttered, "So much," to Sarah's query of, "Anything new?", and hurried off to work before she could satisfy the librarian's curiosity. The diner was quiet enough at first to let her fret over Brent's reappearance, although as the day got busier she was able to let it slip to the back of her mind.

She'd pretty well forgotten about him until her shift was over and she walked out of the diner to find Brent Mitchell waiting for her in the parking lot.

Her heart lurched, and she remembered how it used to be that it would lurch with excitement at seeing him. He was still as good-looking as ever, not as tall as Jake, not as well-built, not as...not as *anything* as Jake Rowly, really. And she could see the meanness around his mouth now in a way she hadn't been able to when she was younger. Now, his presence made her heart clench with dread.

Mabs was surprised at how much she wanted Jake at her side, all of a sudden. Not even to bluster and threaten Brent. Just to be there. Since he wasn't, she just sighed. It was warmer out than it had been that morning. Her breath didn't turn to steam on the air, which was kind of too bad. She might have felt like a dragon, and dragons could no doubt face down ex-boyfriends with ease. "What do you want, Brent?"

"I wanted to know where my family had gone. You look good, Mabs."

"Oh my God." Mabs cast her gaze upward, as if seeking strength from the gathering clouds. "We're not your family. If we were I'd have seen you more than six times since I got pregnant."

He took a few lazy steps closer, like a predator. Mabs's stomach clenched, even though it was daylight and there was a diner full of friends less than a dozen feet behind her. "Aw. c'mon, babe, you know that isn't true. What a crazy thing to say."

A knot of anger formed itself in Mabs's chest. "God, you said that to me all the time. 'What a crazy thing to say'. I don't say crazy things, Brent. I trust myself now, even though you spent so much time trying to make sure I didn't."

His gaze shifted and he almost visibly shifted gears. "Then maybe it's time for me to make amends. What the hell are you doing out at that farm, baby? What the hell was that animal I saw with Noah? Hey, he's a good-looking kid, isn't he? Looks like his daddy."

"What do you really want, Brent? You can't possibly be here to play family, but even if you are, I don't want to anymore. That ship sailed."

"Yeah? You got some other guy up there at that farm? Or did you just leave *my son* alone with a dangerous animal? What was that, a friggin' *wolf*?"

Mabs stared at him flatly. "You mean Wolf? Yes. That's his name."

"You have a wolf named Wolf? I thought you thought you were smart. Oh. I guess the kid named it. I guess he's not all that smart."

Anger pulled Mabs's mouth into a sharp smile. "Well, you're the one who said he's his daddy's son." He hadn't actually said that, but it was close enough to land the hit, and Brent flushed with anger while Mabs shook her head. "He's plenty smart, Brent. He's just a kid. They're pretty literal a lot of the time. Which you might know if you'd spent any time with him. But you haven't, and you're not gonna now. Go back to the city. Whatever reasons you're here aren't good enough."

"That's not how it's going to work, Mabs. We're gonna work this out."

"Dude. Oh my God. That's not how relationships work. Now go the hell home before I call the cops on you for harassment."

"Nobody's going to arrest *me*."

"Maybe not in the city, but there's not a lot around here for the cops to do, Brent. You'd give them something to talk about. Just...go. I don't want to see you again." Mabs sighed. Even more, she didn't want to go to the library to pick Noah up until Brent was gone.

"You gotta introduce him to me, Mabs. My own kid didn't even know who I was."

"Well, that's not my damn fault, Brent. Just...go. I gotta get back to work." She turned and went back into the building, hating the retreat but not seeing much choice.

Her boss, Ross Collins, was leaning on the counter

and had clearly been watching them through the window. "Everything okay, Mabs?"

"Noah's deadbeat dad. I don't want him to know where Noah is right now. Or at all." She took her phone out to text Sarah, explaining she was running late, and a couple seconds later it buzzed with an acknowledgment. In the meantime Ross texted something, too, and Mabs sat down in the back with a soda while customers came in and out. "Is he still out there?" she asked after a while.

Just as she did, a police vehicle's siren went *woop woop* ! and Ross stuck his head into the back to grin. "Not anymore. I called in a complaint about a loiterer. Don't worry, Mabs. We've got your back."

Mabs said, "Thank you," with a whole lot of emotion behind it, and once Brent had been run off, collected Noah, and went home to Jake with a sense of relief.

SHE SAW him before they even got home, up on the roof, continuing the work he'd been doing the day before. A bubble of happiness rose in her and she waved as she got out of the car, smiled foolishly when he waved back, and got Noah out of his car seat feeling much better than she had just a minute earlier. She called, "Don't go anywhere," to the carpenter.

He shouted, "I won't!" back and Mabs was still smiling as she went into the house to get Noah a snack. He sat at the kitchen table with it, pretending he wasn't going to share with Wolf, as Mabs went out to climb the ladder leaning against the buttery roof and stood at the top of it, watching Jake finish nailing a shingle down before saying, "Did Brent come out here again today?"

Jake shook his head, taking several small nails out of his mouth so he could speak. "No. Did you have trouble with him?"

"He came to my work."

Somehow he went from being an interested friend to a worried protector. If he was in his wolf form, Mabs thought, his hackles would rise. "Do you need me to come in and hang around? I don't want him making your life harder, Mabs." For a moment her heart rose, the idea that Jake cared that much helping her mood enormously. Then he said, "You've already got a lot going on with work and Noah and the house and now your classes. Last thing you need is somebody hanging around making it worse."

"I think my job has my back," she said, wishing she had an excuse to have him come hang out, anyway. "My boss called the cops on the stranger loitering in the parking lot."

Jake's smile flashed. "Ross is a good guy. Good. I'm glad. How's Noah?"

"Fine. I just want to keep Brent away from him if I can."

"I'll watch him, if you want to leave him home because Brent's in town."

"Babysitting, carpentry, cooking. Is there anything you don't do, Jake Rowly?"

"I'd say windows, but..." He gestured toward the newly re-framed windows in the wing below them, and Mabs smiled.

"I'm gonna go make dinner. You gonna join us?"

"I'd love to." He eyed the stretch of roof he was looking on. "About how long, do you figure?"

"Half an hour or so?"

"Okay. I can probably get this section done, if I don't screw around. See you in a bit?"

Mabs nodded and went back down the ladder to cook, feeling better for no obvious reason. Dinner came together quickly, with Jake coming in only a few minutes late, having finished shingling and stapling vapor barrier plastic down. "In case the weather changes," he said as he washed his hands. "We've been lucky so far, but at some point the luck's gonna break."

IT BROKE EIGHT HOURS LATER.

Mabs didn't even know what had awakened her: a crash, too loud and also somehow too dull to possibly be Noah. She still jerked out of bed and ran to his room, finding him sprawled unconscious across the bed with Wolf, who wasn't supposed to be *on* the bed. Heart hammering with relief, she flicked the curtains of his windows open, checking to see if something had fallen outside.

Something had.

Snow.

Lots and lots of snow. Inches of it, at least. It piled

on the trees and fences, glowing dimly with light reflected from the single streetlight on her stretch of the main road. Mabs stared at it, disbelieving, then heard Jake's footsteps on the stairs and left Noah's room to meet him.

He was barefoot, in a white t-shirt and plaid sleeping pants, and cold was blowing in from somewhere. Mabs blinked at his outfit, too surprised to think about the snow for a moment. "You change into pajamas to sleep?"

He looked at himself, and back at her, his eyebrows crinkled in confusion. "Don't most people?"

"I guess, but I thought you were sleeping as a wolf, and your clothes change with you, so I guess I...I dunno. I guess I didn't think about you changing to sleep."

"Ah." Jake's shoulders shook with contained laughter. "I spent a summer when I was about nine working under logic kind of like that. I figured if I just slept as a wolf then it somehow made it okay to be wearing the same clothes the next day. It took Mom a while to notice, but when she did I got read the riot act and dumped in the bath. Including my shoes. So now I change clothes to sleep in, even if I'm sleeping as a wolf."

"Oh my God. Kids are so gross."

"They really are." Jake exhaled, his breath suddenly visible in the air. "I'm afraid to open the bedroom doors."

"I don't know if you looked outside. It snowed," Mabs said grimly. "So we kind of have to, though, don't we?" Three of the upstairs bedrooms were over the parlor half of the house, two on the house's front and one large one overlooking the back garden. A hall separated them. Mabs edged down that hall, nervously pushing one of the front bedrooms' doors open. She didn't know what to expect under the best of circumstances, having barely even looked into the rooms since moving in.

It looked fine. She frowned, glanced at Jake, and went down the hall to check the other front bedroom, then opened the door to the larger back bedroom. Everything looked normal, for the value of 'normal' that involved rooms having gone untouched for decades. She exchanged another glance with Jake as she came back to the upstairs landing, and they both looked up.

"I haven't been in the attic," Mabs said warily. "I'm not sure how to *get* in the attic." That wasn't entirely true. There was an entrance...door, or whatever the appropriate term for a covered hole in a ceiling was, at the far end of the hall. A cord dangled down from it, but Mabs wasn't even tall enough to reach it, which had been a pretty great excuse for not even bothering to look up there.

Jake, luckily—or not—was tall enough to reach it easily, and pulled it open. Rickety stairs unfolded, and a blast of absolutely freezing air rolled down, making Mabs shiver from the bones out. "That can't be good."

"Nope." Jake went up first, which was chivalrous. Mabs stayed on the floor, looking, if she was to be perfectly honest about things, at his butt in the thin sleeping pants, which was a pretty good view. He stopped with his head and shoulders in the attic, so she couldn't follow him anyway, and said a word that Noah would inform him wasn't appropriate for children to hear. He turned and down the ladder a couple of steps, leaning one hand inside the attic and peering down at Mabs with a pained smile. "Do you want to build a snowman?"

"What? *What?*" Mabs climbed the ladder, squeezing past Jake, which under other circumstances would have been *amazing*, and stopped still more or less within the circle of his arms to stare around the attic in dismay.

The main, swayback beam of the roof had broken under the weight of more snow than she could even imagine falling at once. Splintered wood poked out of what looked like whole *feet* of snow inside the attic, its brightness reflecting light from the clouds visible through the hole in the roof. "Oh my God. Oh no." She sank back a little, into Jake's warmth, and fought off a wave of despair mixed powerfully with a wave of desire.

His hands tightened around the staircase handles as she leaned into him, and he murmured, "Careful," against her hair. "It'll be all right. We'll get it fixed, Mabs. Lemme go get my gear and I'll get up on the roof and seal it off. You can—can you get some buckets? A shovel? To clean up the snow so it doesn't leak through to the bedrooms?"

"Yeah. Okay." She turned like she'd go down a regular set of stairs, and found herself nose to nose with the carpenter. "Oh. Uh. Hi. Sorry."

He smiled, almost against her mouth. "Hi. How's it going?"

"Pretty good." Very good, actually, given how wonderful he smelled, and the sparkle in his eyes, and the thinness of his clothes and hers. Then an icy breeze dropped straight down Mabs's back and she yelped. "Except my butt is freezing off."

"Well, we can't have that." Jake hopped off the ladder and offered her a hand, which she took despite not needing help. His fingers were warm and strong, and hers were surprisingly cold, given that she'd really only been out of bed for about three minutes. She shivered as she stepped down to the floor and told herself it was probably the cold, and not Jake's touch, sending trembles over her. "You'd better get a coat and boots," he said, which seemed sensible, if not nearly as much fun as other ways she could think of to warm up.

On the other hand, no amount of fun was going to take care of the *hole* in her *roof*, or the *giant pile of snow* in her *attic*, so she guessed maybe a coat and boots were the smart choice after all. Jake went downstairs to get his tools. Mabs followed, trying not to think about the various implications *tools* carried, and wondered why she was so horny in the freezing cold middle of the night.

Twenty minutes later, shoveling snow out of her attic, she decided horny was better than grumpy, but it was too late by then.

CHAPTER 16

$\mathcal{J}$ ake felt like an idiot.

He straight-up hadn't checked the roof of what Mabs called "the parlor side of the house". He'd known the beam was weak, of course: it was visible from the outside of the house. But like Mabs, he'd barely been in the parlor side, concentrating on the half she and Noah were actually living in. Still, if he'd even so much as gone up, instead of just talking about it, he might have realized how weak it *was*, and done something about it.

In his defense, it rarely snowed in November, and he couldn't remember an early snowfall heavy enough to break a roof in his whole life. On the other hand, weather patterns had changed dramatically since he was a kid, so he guessed anything was possible.

Obviously anything was possible. He said it to himself before his wolf could, and got a snort in response.

I wasn't going to say that. Which was probably true. It

wasn't really the kind of thing the wolf *did* say. Things were, or were not, from a wolf's point of view. Possible and impossible didn't really come into it.

Jake was, he realized, essentially having an imaginary argument with his wolf, who was, from almost anybody else's point of view, imaginary anyway.

Not if I bite them, I'm not.

A low chuckle rolled out of Jake's chest. "Yeah. Yeah, I know. All right." He got the ladder, a snow shovel, vapor barrier, and the staple gun, and went up on the roof to apply them all in the appropriate order. Mabs, inside the attic, had wrestled one of the windows open and was shoveling snow out of it. They worked in relative silence, not wanting to wake Noah, and within an hour or so the roof was sealed enough to make it until morning, and the attic was clear of snow.

Mabs went downstairs while Jake cleaned up the tools of his trade, and when he came into the kitchen, found her in the kitchen, still wearing her giant boots as she poured cocoa into mugs. "I know it's four in the morning," she said in warning tones. "We're having hot chocolate anyway. We deserve it."

"I would never argue with the lady of the house."

"Good." She gave him a smile that was both stern and playful, and Jake's stomach flip-flopped. She was everything he could imagine wanting in a partner: smart, funny, sexy as hell, strong, independent, willing to accept help, crazy-competent, ambitious, gorgeous, able to put in hard work in the middle of the night—

—which sounded much, much dirtier than he'd

meant it to. Mabs put a sprinkle of cinnamon on top of the cocoa and handed him a mug.

"Trust me," she said at his dubious look, and he sipped to discover that she was, as it turned out, also very good at making hot chocolate. "Toldja," she said, satisfied, and sat down to draw her feet up on a chair and hold her mug over her knees. "So you remember how you thought you should take care of the parlor-side roof and I suggested doing the buttery instead?"

Jake sat too, eyebrows rising. "Yeah?"

"I've decided you were right."

Surprise caught him off guard and he laughed. "Oh yeah?"

"Yeah. Too bad I didn't trust the actual carpenter in the first place."

"You weren't wrong about the shingles, though. There were just enough for the buttery wing." He pulled a face. "Which I'm going to have to clear off and finish, like, yesterday. I don't want it leaking in the house."

Mabs sighed deeply into her mug. "There's a lot of things I don't want, and yet here we are."

"Like what?" His voice softened, but a protective instinct rose in him, as if he could fend off whatever it was that bothered her.

"Oh, you know. A hole in my roof. An ex-boyfriend showing up in town. A bank account veering toward negative numbers. The usual. Crap," she added, looking tired all of a sudden. "I wonder if I should cancel Thanksgiving. There's only a couple people coming anyway, but I wasn't planning to have snow falling in half the house."

"Noah would actually implode with disappointment," Jake pointed out, and earned a wry smile in return.

"That's true. Well, it wasn't going to be a big deal anyway. Maybe if we just really seal that half of the house off it'll be okay?"

"It'll be fine," Jake promised, and meant it. "Do you need help in the kitchen?"

Mabs looked toward the Aga like it might suddenly require maintenance. "Not right now, thanks." She slid a smile at him, though, and said, "Tomorrow maybe, though. I have to make a couple of pies before Thursday morning. Noah's gonna wanna help, which will make it take about fifteen times longer, so I might put you to work, but...probably Visqueening the entire right-hand side of the house is more important."

"Want me to Visqueen Noah, too?"

Mabs laughed. "No, not at the moment. I make no guarantees about tomorrow, mind you, but not today. Anyway, uh, sorry my house fell apart on us in the middle of the night, I'd give you the day off tomorrow, but..."

"Oh, don't worry about it, I had a day off last month," Jake assured her. "I even had a date with a goddess."

"Daaaang. I'd better up my game." Mabs's eyebrows drew down a little, like she didn't know why she'd said that, or where to go from there. Then she shook it off, almost like his wolf would do, and smiled. "Right. Do you think we should put up some more plastic upstairs? Over the doors, anyway?"

Jake wrinkled his face, looking toward the upstairs. "Probably a good idea, if we can do it quietly enough to keep from waking Noah. It'll get pretty damn cold in here otherwise."

"I have about sixty rolls of double-sided tape," Mabs suggested. "That would probably hold it overnight, at least?"

"Probably." Jake waited several seconds, sipping his cocoa, then couldn't stand it anymore. "*Why* do you have sixty rolls of double-sided tape..."

Mabs shook her head. "It involved a terrible incident with a toddler, an open browser window, and a non-refundable purchase on eBay."

Jake laughed. "Oh. Oh no."

"You have no idea." Mabs drained the rest of her cocoa, rose, stretched, and pulled her winter coat back on. "Okay. I'm gonna go get tape, and then you can be strong and tall and handsome and do all the high parts while I go low."

"I have no objections to being considered tall and strong and handsome, but I'm using a stepladder so my arms don't go numb." Jake stood, finishing his own cocoa, and Mabs grinned.

"Tall, strong, handsome, and smart. I'm going to have to keep you around."

Jake's heart thumped and he tried not to smile too idiotically. The idea that she *wanted* to keep him around warmed him until he thought he might need to take his winter coat off. "We've got renovation plans through next spring. Good luck getting rid of me before then."

"I wasn't going to try," she promised, then bounded up the stairs like a more grown-up version of Noah, as if the hot chocolate had energized her. The next hour or so was spent taping vapor barrier up, with Mabs swearing more creatively than he'd ever heard, especially when the tape insisted on sticking to itself instead of the walls and Visqueen. He kept whispering, "Shh!" and she would *shh!* him back, until they both had to stop putting plastic up and sit down, hands over their mouths to contain giggles.

This, Jake thought, looking at her eyes shining with laughter, at her sleep-and-sweat-mussed hair, at the big bundled coat and heavy winter boots, and the totally inadequate pajama bottoms between them, *this* was what he wanted. Nothing could be sweeter, or more satisfying, than days and nights spent with her. Even if they were nights of cleaning up snowfall inside a house, nothing could be better.

Smiling, he looked up at the job they'd done, and said, "This will probably hold until morning. I'll do a better job then. It's late. You should get back to bed."

"Ugh." Mabs made a face. "Cold bed. I mean, I guess at least it's not snowy, but I was comfy before. Whiii-ine." She actually said that, then laughed at herself.

"Well, I could—" Jake nearly swallowed his tongue and Mabs's eyebrows shot up.

"You could what?"

"Um. Nothing appropriate."

Her eyebrows rose even higher. "Well, now you *have* to tell me."

"It wasn't *that* inappropriate. I just—I was going to say—aaah, no, never mind." He couldn't say what had leaped to mind without it sounding like something entirely different.

Mabs, though, bundled in her coat and big boots over her pajamas, gave him an amused look. "Gonna say what?"

"This is going to come out all wrong," he warned her, and her amusement increased toward curious laughter.

"I promise not to get offended, if that helps. What?"

"I was going to say I could sleep with you. As a wolf!" he added hastily. "I'm really warm and I have a built-in fur coat. I'd keep the draft off..." By the end of that he wanted to bury his head in a hole, it sounded so awful and self-serving.

On the other hand, Mabs had turned a delicious shade of pink at his first sentence, and had just maybe been disappointed when he'd added *as a wolf!* She wet her lips, looked at the weather barrier plastic they'd put up, looked at her bedroom door, and looked back at Jake. "Noah's got Wolf," she said a little hoarsely. "I guess I could use a wolf of my own?"

"Really?" His voice cracked and he cleared his throat, trying to sound even slightly dignified. "I mean...really?"

"Really." She'd turned so very pink. Jake wondered how low the blush went, and told himself that was *not* what he should be thinking just then. He was *not* trying to flirt with her.

His wolf woke up and stared at him as if he was the most useless person on the face of the planet, turned around, lay back down, and went back to sleep in obvious disapproval. Mabs, still pink, kept talking, although she seemed to be having a little trouble with words herself. "Really. It'd be nice to have...somebody warm...in the bed? Oh, God, is this too weird? It's too weird, I should shut up."

Jake held his hands up, smiling. "No weirdness," he promised. "Large good-natured canine, no weirdness. I swear. Look, here." He shifted into a wolf and lay down, chin on his paws and his tail thumping hopefully.

"Aw, you're so cute." Mabs leaned over to scritch the top of his head, said, "I mean, you gotta admit, this is a *little* weird," and went into her room with Jake trotting along behind her.

CHAPTER 17

No weirdness, because Jake shifting into a wolf before coming into Mabs's bedroom was definitely not weird. And it was probably a good idea, overall.

Probably.

Maybe.

No, definitely good. Even though all she was undressing from was her winter coat and boots, it would have been really strange doing that while Jake-the-human watched. Or maybe not strange. Not sexy, either, though, because she was wearing a winter coat, for heaven's sake, and huge boots. Mabs couldn't think of any scenario where undressing from that was anything other than faintly humorous, at best.

And really, Jake just acted like a big dog, although honestly, Mabs had never met a dog with as much presence as the wolf had. Even knowing he was human, too, he was so... *wild*. Self-assured. No one could mistake him for a mere dog, even if true wolves didn't have blue eyes.

Regardless, he pretended to be a dog, and hopped up on her bed with the confidence of a long-time canine companion. He even turned around on it a couple of times before lying down, politely, with his back to her while she pulled off her boots and coat.

Not until she got *on* the bed did she suddenly, for the first time, appreciate how damn *big* he was. Wolves were big, and Mabs guessed Jake was probably bigger than average, because he was tall and strongly built, and while his clothes shifted with him, his mass didn't seem to change at all when he changed shape.

His *shape* did, though, which: obviously. But wolves and humans weren't built on the same frame, and even though he'd curled up tidily like a polite dog, he still took up *more than half the bed.* Mabs, suddenly grinning, pushed him as she tried to crawl under the covers. "Move over, you big lunk."

Jake lifted his head and gave her the most positively mournful puppy dog eyes she'd ever seen, and conceded half an inch of bed to her. She pushed harder. "Scoot!"

Sigh. *Siiiiiigh.* He moved another couple of inches, then rolled far enough onto his back to not only take back all the space she'd reclaimed, but to give her upside-down puppy eyes, his front feet flopping loosely in the air.

"Oh my God." Mabs rubbed his belly, then pushed him to the side again. "Scoot, or I'll make you sleep on the floor."

"Would you really?" Jake shifted between one push and another, capturing her hand against his ribs.

Mabs's brain shut down. It was one thing to have a blue-eyed silver wolf in her bed. It was something else *entirely* to have a blue-eyed silver *fox* in her bed, as it were, and Jake Rowly was *so. damned. attractive.*

"That's not..." Her voice had disappeared, along with whatever brain cells she had to rub together. He was *right* there, and she was only in pajamas. Not sexy ones, either, but lumpy flannel that kept her warm, but still, pajamas, and he was *right* there, with an absolutely devastating little grin only a few inches away from her mouth, and his eyes bright and sparkling as he looked at her.

What was left of her voice broke as she said, "...fair. That's not fair."

Sudden dismay crashed across his face and he backed up, all the wicked humor drowned in apology. "No, you're right, it really wasn't. I'm sorry, Mabs. I don't usually—people don't usually talk to me when I'm a wolf. I just wanted to answer. I didn't think. I'm sorry." He'd backed up so far he had to catch himself on the edge of the bed, and all at once he turned to swing his feet to the floor. "I'd better go."

Mabs reached across the bed to touch the small of his back with her fingertips. The muscle there tensed, and she had to curl her fingers back again to keep from spreading her hand across the warmth of his spine. "You don't have to go." Her voice still barely existed. "Just...pick a shape and stick with it. Please."

His breath caught and he turned his head, showing

her his profile in the dim bedroom light. He was so, so gorgeous, and he looked so, so nervous all of a sudden. His voice was even lower than her own, hardly even a whisper. "Do you have a preference for which shape?"

Sheer horny adrenaline spiked through Mabs, turning her hands cold and other parts of her tinglingly hot. "Yeah." She swallowed and reached for his back again, hands trembling with the effort. "I like this one."

"Mabs." Jake turned so fast she hardly saw him move, but she certainly felt the warmth of his hands on her waist as he pulled her up and toward him, almost into his lap. Her pulse skyrocketed so sharply she got dizzy and gave a breathless laugh, one that he almost swallowed without quite closing a kiss. "Mabs, are you sure?"

"So sure. Very sure. Sure-er than anything."

He lifted his hands to her cheeks, murmured, "Mabs," and lowered his mouth to hers. Soft lips at first, barely parted, then opening, exchanging breath, exploring shapes, learning how their mouths fit together, until Mabs's whole body was on fire, need coursing through her blood and electrifying every part of her. She whimpered, sliding her hands into his hair, opening her mouth farther to his, and her desire was met by his answering groan.

She kept her hands in his hair as his slid to her hips, pulling her firmly into his lap. Mabs was suddenly glad she *was* wearing only pajamas, even if they weren't pretty ones, because it wouldn't take any real effort to get them out of the way and she suddenly wanted them out of the way very, very badly. Jake's hands rose from her hips, ruffling the edge of her pajama tops upward. His thumbs brushed the lower curve of her breasts and she cried out into his mouth, a sound of hope.

Bizarrely, he pulled sharply away, sudden panic in his face as Mabs tried, through a blaze of desire, to focus on him. Before she could even say his name, he suddenly twisted away, dumped her on the bed, and shapeshifted into a wolf.

Less than a heartbeat later, Noah, carrying his puppy, opened the door and said, "Mommy? It's cold in my room and there's snow in the hall," miserably. "Can Wolf and I sleep with you and Mr. Growly?"

Mabs dropped her chin to her chest and took three seconds to absolutely quiver with frustration, then dared to glance sideways at Jake.

Dogs did guilty looks well, but she'd never seen *rueful* on a canine face before. He shrugged and lay down with his head on his paws, no longer taking up two-thirds of the bed. Mabs whispered "Visqueen" at him, and his mouth pulled back in a broad, wolfy grin before he gave a huff that sounded an awful lot like laughter.

Mabs, with a rueful sigh of her own, pulled the covers back as she turned her attention back to Noah. "Of course, baby. Some of the roof fell down on the other side of the house. Mr. Rowly and I will get it fixed up soon so it'll be warmer, but until then..." She could just about die, saying this, but her kid not freezing was kind of more important than getting laid. "Until then you can sleep in my room, if you want."

"Okay." Noah flopped into bed with Wolf tucked

under his chin, and went back to sleep instantly. Mabs lay down beside them, staring at the ceiling. Jake gently rested his furry chin on her shoulder and licked her ear, which under other circumstances might have been very sexy, but in this one—

—in this one, it made Mabs laugh. She rolled halfway over, hugged Jake's furry shoulders, and to her own surprise, went to sleep pretty quickly herself.

WAKING up in a lump of furry bodies and cute little boy was, Mabs had to admit, maybe the nicest thing she'd ever done. Nice enough that she really didn't want to get up, but the alarm was going off and she had a work shift to make. She groaned, crawled over Jake, who lifted his big furry head, looked around blearily, and flopped back down on the pillow, exactly like a large dog, and changed her mind as soon as she got out of the bed, because it was *freezing* in the house. She whispered, "Oh my God," and jammed her boots back on to go peek out the window.

There'd been enough snow the night before to crack the roof, but it hadn't let up then. There had to be over a foot, maybe eighteen inches, piled brilliantly across the front yard, stacked on the fence, burying her car, burying everything in sight.

Noah thumped out of bed behind her, staggered to the window, stared, screamed, "SNOW, MOMMY! *SNOW* !!!" and ran straight out of her room, down the stairs, and out the front door.

Mabs waited.

Five seconds later Noah burst back into the house, shrieking, "It's cold it's cold it's cold Mommy it's COLD!" She could hear him finding shoes, if not a coat, and a moment later he went tearing back out into the snow again, Wolf now leaping at his heels.

Jake, tall and handsome and very human, padded up beside her to push the curtain farther open and squint at the snow. "Wow."

"Right?" Mabs wanted very badly to lean back against him, and bit her lip to keep herself from doing so. *Probably* it would be okay, but one exceedingly hot kiss did not a boyfriend make, and leaning on guys was kind of boyfriend-level activity. "I don't think I'm going to work today."

"MOMMY!" Noah came pounding back into the house and ran up the stairs into her room, shedding snow all the way. "It's *cold* outside!"

"Maybe you should get dressed, honey."

"I am dressed!"

"You're wearing pajamas and sneakers. You could try warm clothes, boots, and a coat."

He stared at her, nonplussed, and marched back out again, not, Mabs suspected, to find appropriate clothing. Wolf skidded in, spun around, and ran back out after his boy, leaving Mabs and Jake to both smile after them. Then Jake said, "It's freezing in here," and Mabs sighed.

"Yeah, I noticed. We're gonna have to...I don't even know what."

"It's okay. I do." Jake kissed her hair like it was the

natural thing to do and left her grinning like an idiot in her bedroom. A few minutes later, as she was getting dressed, she heard Noah yelling gleefully, and looked out the window to see Jake throwing shovels-ful of snow off the roof and it falling in poofs around Noah.

If there wasn't a giant hole in the roof and no money in the bank account, Mabs thought, it would be a pretty perfect life. It came surprisingly close anyway.

She called work to say she was snowed in—"Better than calling in sick, worse than calling in rich," her boss said cheerfully, but the diner was closed anyway because most of the staff couldn't get there until the roads were cleared—and spent the day alternating between Thanksgiving preparations, helping Jake hang the vapor barrier better, and chasing both Noah and Wolf out of the kitchen.

"It's not going to be warm," Jake said mid-afternoon, after half the house was as well sealed-off as they could make it. "I'm sorry, Mabs. And the forecast is calling for more snow. I can go pick up some plywood to nail over the hole, once the roads clear. In the meantime, we might want to get everything out of those rooms, if we can."

"The rooms we just sealed up with three layers of heavy plastic?"

"My timing may not be great," Jake admitted. He smelled fresh and snowy and delicious. Better, Mabs thought, than the pies she had baked, although it probably wasn't *super* appropriate to suggest eating him with some whipped cream.

Not where Noah might overhear, anyway. Heat

crawled up Mabs's cheeks and she tried hard to pretend she hadn't made herself blush.

Jake lifted his eyebrows at her, before his expression softened into something she didn't quite understand. "Bad timing," he said, not quite repeating himself. "Right. Tell you what, I'm going to check the barn and see if there's anything out there I can use to patch up the roof for a few days, at least, until the snow melts. It can't stay until March." The last words sounded more like a question than a confident statement.

"Oh, God, I hope not. Could it? We'll freeze."

Jake's smile gentled even more. "You both have wolves to keep you warm."

Jake liked to think he could take a hint, disappointing as it might be. But Mabs had reacted pretty strongly to 'my timing may not be great,' and Jake realized he had nothing but time. Time holed up in a snowbound house sounded perfect, in fact, and it would be good for Mabs to have a couple of comparatively down days, if she could let herself. He would certainly try to make that easier, anyway, even if some of the most tension-releasing activities he could think of seemed off the table for now.

He might have worked a little tension off himself by repairing the roof, but the truth was there wasn't much in the barn that could do the trick. The house did warm up some with three layers of plastic holding the cold back, but he really wanted to fix it, as if...

...as if fixing the fallen roof could somehow show Mabs he had every intention—every hope—of sticking around. He'd said he would a hundred times already, but they were always light comments about finishing some bit of project *next year*, and he knew it must be easy to not take that seriously. He wanted to find a way to tell her he really was reliable, that he wanted to be there, without also scaring her off—

*Just **tell** her!*

—and the best way he knew how to do that was to keep showing her, by being there.

And maybe by eating more Thanksgiving dinner than he had since he was fifteen, but that, he thought, sated, at the end of the next day, was only because Mabs was an amazing cook.

Nobody else had made it over for the holiday, not with the roads in the condition they were, so there had been far too much food for three. Or even four, if he counted Wolf, whose appetite for turkey certainly *wanted* to be counted.

"The good news is I won't have to cook again for a week," Mabs said after she'd put Noah to bed. "The bad news is we're all gonna be sick of turkey in three days."

"My mom used to freeze whole turkey dinners after Thanksgiving," Jake suggested. "She portioned up the gravy, the turkey, some cranberry sauce—"

"That was *amazing* cranberry sauce," Mabs interrupted. "Was that her recipe? Will you share it with me?"

"It was and I will, or I can just keep making it for you." Jake was cleaning the kitchen as he spoke, and cast a glance to see how that had landed.

Pretty well, from her smile, although she glanced down and wouldn't meet his gaze. He ducked his head and went back to cleaning the kitchen. "Anyway, basically everything that could get frozen, she froze in meal-sized portions and then we'd get to have random Thanksgiving dinners in April. It was great."

"I'll have to do that. Tomorrow," she said, glancing at the fridge, where more food than seemed possible had been stuffed. "I'm not taking that all out again and repackaging it tonight."

"Plenty of time. We won't be sick of leftovers by tomorrow." He reached up above one of the cupboards, taking down a bottle of wine, and lifted his eyebrows at Mabs curiously.

"Where'd *that* come from? Don't tell me it's been here since I moved in. I could've used it a time or two." She stood on her toes, stretching her neck like she could possibly see the tops of the shelves, and sighed. "I need those to be six inches lower. Ugh, tall people. It must be nice to be tall people."

"I bought it earlier in the week," Jake promised. "It hasn't been up there taunting you. And I'd be glad to be tall for you whenever you need."

Her smile blossomed. "Thanks. Why don't you be tall and get a couple of wine glasses down, then? I'd love a glass. Leave the dishes," she said, almost as impe-rious as Noah could be. "They can wait for a glass of wine."

"Your wish is my command." There *were* wine glasses at the back of one of the higher shelves, crystal that Jake thought was probably older than he was. He took a couple down, rinsed them, and patted them dry before pouring first Mabs, then himself, a glass of wine. Then he lifted his toward hers in a toast. "To your first Thanksgiving in the Old Brannigan Place."

"May it be the first of many." Mabs sipped her wine, brows lifting a little in appreciation. "Oh, that's nice. Thanks." She met his eyes over the wine glasses. "For everything, Jake."

"What are friends for?"

"Man, friends are for helping you move, and best friends are for helping you move the body. I don't even know where 'rebuild your entire house for the cost of a couch to sleep on' falls into that."

"...'move the body'... Is there something I should know?"

Mabs laughed. "No. Jeez. No. It's a joke."

"Just checking." They shared the wine over an hour or so, doing dishes between glasses, until Jake realized Mabs's eyes were drifting closed as they sat chatting. Half a bottle of wine didn't have much effect on him, but he hadn't thought what it might do to somebody eight inches shorter and probably sixty pounds lighter than he was. "C'mon," he said gently. "Let's get you upstairs before you fall asleep."

Mabs chuckled and said, "Okay," agreeably, then leaned on him as he guided her up the stairs. She didn't bother brushing her teeth or even undressing, for that matter, just fell face-first onto her bed and put a hand out, mumbling, "Jake?"

"Yeah?"

"Stay?"

He smiled, murmured, "Yeah," and shifted as he crawled onto the bed with her. She put her arm around him, buried her nose in his fur, and slept so quickly, so soundly, that he knew she felt safe.

And that, he realized, was all he wanted.

THE SOUND of dripping woke him up before dawn. He hopped out of bed, claws clicking on the floor until he got to the door, which needed human hands to open, and went downstairs to look for the source of the drips.

It turned out to be 'the world,' which had thawed overnight. The house was warmer, and the front yard had turned to crunchy melting snow, shrinking almost visibly as he watched. The roads were going to be terrible with ice and melt, but by tomorrow, at the latest, Mabs would be able to get back to work.

Which didn't sound nearly as appealing as her being at the house with Jake, but did, he admitted, bear some relevance on paying the bills. He knew Mabs felt like she was taking advantage of him, but the funny thing was, he felt like he was taking advantage of her, too. He'd had a warm, safe place to live for months now, and no bills to worry about. No income, either, true, but he hadn't really needed any.

He went around the house, checking out the roof now that the snow was melting, and cringed as he saw the wind had taken up a flap of the plastic. Some of that dripping might be in the house after all. With a sigh, Jake went up on the roof, first to nail down the plastic on the parlor side of the house, then to clear the roof on the buttery. There really wasn't much left to do there, so he got to work, hoping to finish the shingling before nightfall.

After lunch, around mid-afternoon, a car bumped up along the slushy road, finding potholes that Jake was pretty sure hadn't been there a couple days earlier. He put the hammer down and sat on his butt, watching, in case they needed help, but instead of driving by, the car pulled up to Mabs's gate, and the wolf within Jake growled.

He was already on his way off the roof when he heard Mabs say, "Jake? I don't know if you've got wolf hearing when you're a human, but if you could come in here and just keep Noah busy while I deal with this, I'd really appreciate it."

He had, he realized then, had every intention of confronting Brent Mitchell, who was getting out of his car now. The simple fact that Mabs needed him to do something else—to protect her child—changed everything for him. *Everything*. The realization that she trusted him that much, that she relied on him—Jake knew he probably shouldn't be grinning like a fool when he came in through the back door, but he was. Mabs needed him to do something much more important than help her stand her ground, and nothing else mattered.

She was standing at her front door, one hand knotted around the knob, tension in her shoulders until he said, "I'm here," from behind her. Then all her tension unwound and she smiled radiantly over her shoulder at him. "You heard me?"

"Wolves have good hearing."

She grinned, spun toward him, took the few steps that separated them, and pressed a sweet, swift kiss against his lips. "I love you."

Then she raced outside, while Jake's knees buckled and he stared after her, gobsmacked, before going to keep an eye on Noah in the living room.

CHAPTER 19

*M*abs heard the irretrievable words leave her mouth after it was too late: *I love you*. That was not the kind of thing you just went around saying to fantastically hot carpenters who were rebuilding your house, but God damn if it wasn't true. It *was* true. She didn't know how that had happened, or when. In between all the lusting and longing and puppy dog eyes, she guessed, and the phrase *puppy dog eyes* was, in the end, so accurate, that she was actually giggling when she went out of the house to see what the hell her ex wanted.

Brent hadn't actually come through the gate, but he was standing right at it, arms akimbo, his gaze fixed on the giant hole in the farmhouse roof. "What the fuck, Mabs."

All of a sudden Mabs really just couldn't remember what had made Brent attractive in the first place. She stopped several feet away, arms crossed, and kind of shook her head at him. "Hi, how are you, fine, thanks, how's it going? Jesus, Brent, what's wrong with you?"

"Me? What's wrong with *you*, moving to the middle of nowhere into a falling-apart money pit? Taking my kid up here without even telling me? That's kidnapping! I'm gonna take him back, Mabs! You can't raise my son in these conditions!"

Mabs couldn't even manage a scowl. She was just incredulous, staring at him in his nice wool coat and his glare that wiped out whatever had once been handsome about him. "What's Noah's middle name, Brent?"

"What? What does that have to do with anything?" At least he stopped glaring at the roof and turned his attention to her, his face curled with confusion.

She dismissed the question with a downturn of her lips. "Nothing. I don't owe you any explanations, Brent. Go back to the city, get on with your life. I don't know how you found us, but it was a waste of your time."

"I've got friends who let me know things," Brent sneered. "Besides, what was I supposed to do? You disappeared with my kid—"

"As if he's ever mattered to you!"

Brent kept talking like she hadn't spoken. "And now you're living in a dump. You should sell the place and come back to the city with me. I bet you could get a mint for it. There's gotta be a local realtor around here who could do you a nice deal. It's a nice piece of land here, there must be somebody who wants it." He suddenly changed his tone, sounding cajoling now. Or at least more cajoling than he had, but Mabs thought it sounded like a performance.

A performance that didn't make any sense. She shook her head, honestly confused. "What, did your folks cut off the trust fund or something and you need a sugar mama? Brent, if we'd stayed together I'd have done anything to help you, but you dumped me when I was four months pregnant. What exactly do you imagine I'm going to do here, throw myself at your feet and be grateful you've decided to take me back?"

"I've got to be better than this place! Seriously, Mabs, look at it. It's falling apart." Brent produced a winsome smile that reminded her enormously of Noah trying to wheedle something out of her. Only with less emotional integrity, which was saying a lot, since Noah's efforts tended to be incredibly transparent.

"We don't live in that half of the house, Brent," she said wearily, hoping that offering some information would get him off her back. "Not right now, anyway. I'm planning repairs for it next summer. Just...go back to the city."

"Oh, so you've got all that space and you're not even using it? That's wasteful, isn't it? More than that, there's wild animals around here, Mabs, you gotta know that. Noah's not safe in a place like this."

Mabs thought about Jake, and his very large sharp teeth, and decided it would be wrong, wrong, *wrong* to call him out here and have him show Brent his teeth. Tempting, but wrong. She bet he'd love to do it, though, and a little grin started pulling at her mouth.

Brent saw it and flushed with anger. "What, you think I'm not taking my son's safety seriously?"

"I think you've never visited, paid child support, or

shown any interest in him, so, yeah, I kinda think you're not taking it very seriously. Brent, just...go home."

"I'll sue for custody, Mabs." Brent's voice dropped dangerously, but the threat was so ridiculous that she just frowned in disbelief.

At some point in the past, Mabs knew she would have felt threatened by the idea, but...things were different now. She had a safe home, one that she wouldn't lose to a landlord. She had a community of friends, a reliable paycheck, and classes toward the job she'd always *wanted*.

She had Jake Rowly.

She had Jake, and the fact that he was inside, protecting her son, letting her fight her own battles, *trusting* her.... She hadn't realized how badly she needed to trust herself, how badly, maybe, she needed someone *else* to trust her, to help her regain her belief in herself. She'd been confident, when she was younger. At some point—while she was with Brent—that had disappeared.

Mabs did not, for a minute, believe that Jake Rowly had *made* her confident again. He'd just looked at her, and treated her, like she was amazing, *all the time*, until she'd started believing it again herself.

Somehow, *somehow*, a little smile appeared on her face. "Okay, Brent. You go ahead and try that. Just...yeah. You go do that. Sue for custody. That'll be fun."

His face darkened. "Don't think I won't!"

"I think you will." Mabs took a deep, soothing

breath, and exhaled it as a cloud of steam. "I'm just not too worried about it."

He pointed a finger at her, almost shaking with rage. "You're gonna regret this, Mabs."

"I guess we'll see." Mabs lifted her chin, pointing toward his car with it. "You can see yourself off my property now. I'd hate to bother the sheriff on the holiday weekend."

"You wouldn't."

Mabs, with a sigh, pulled her phone out of her hip pocket, and Brent, swearing, bolted for his car. "This place is a fire hazard, Mabs! I'm gonna get custody and then you'll be sorry!"

"You should grow a mustache so you can twirl it!" Mabs held her ground until he'd driven away, then staggered back to the porch to collapse into its swing for a minute.

Or three. Or five. She was just gathering herself to get up when Jake opened the door and peeked out, his expression cautiously concerned. "You okay?"

"I am. I...yeah. I think I am."

Jake slipped out, closing the door behind him, and offered a guilty look. "I gave Noah my phone."

Mabs laughed, a little ratta-tat-tat sound that turned into a bigger laugh. "Surefire way to distract him. Straight out of Parenting 101. Thank you." She sat up and reached for Jake's hand as he approached. "I couldn't wrangle Noah and deal with Brent at the same time."

"Any time." He ran his thumb over her knuckles and

sat beside her on the swing, searching her gaze. "You're sure you're all right? He was being a dick."

"I'm sure. Yeah, I'm sure." His hand was so warm around Mabs's that she looked down to see if somehow they'd caught fire. They hadn't, of course, but she liked the look of her hand in his. "Look, I, um, since Noah's distracted anyway I should probably say something about, um, what I said in there. Before I came outside."

"You don't have to." He spoke quietly, expression kind. "People do say that kind of thing when they're relieved at getting unexpected help."

"I guess so, but I meant it." Mabs bit her lower lip and nerved herself up to meet Jake's blue eyes. "And I know you're not looking for a relationship, that you came back to Virtue because there weren't any possibilities here, so I just—I want you to know if you think you might ever be interested...I could wait a while. I'd like to wa—"

Jake's free hand came up to cup her cheek and he kissed her. Just enough to stop her words, at first, and then he loosened his other hand to cup the other side of her face, his warm touch melting her as his lips brushed hers again, then again, deepening. She was breathless when he backed away just enough to rest his forehead against hers and whispered, "I don't want to wait. I love you too."

"Oh—oh! Really?" Mabs bit her lip, a smile so big it brought on tears threatening to overwhelm her. "Really?"

"Since the minute I saw you," Jake admitted quietly. "I've been denying it to myself because you—well, you have a lot going on, and some random guy showing up and being moon-eyed didn't seem...good."

Mabs thought her heart would actually soar from her chest with joy. "Technically you're right but oh my God, Jake, you walked into my life like a...not like a hurricane."

"You already have one of those."

She laughed, tears spilling over. "Yeah. Yeah, I do. Honestly, though, you were just the most gorgeous guy, and you...wanted to help, and...you mean I've been nursing a crush all these months when we could've been sleeping together instead?" She sat up, still smiling like an idiot, and knocked her shoulder against his. "What a waste of time!"

"Nah." He chased her with a kiss, his mouth hungry on hers as his hands found her waist. He lifted her into his lap with ease, nuzzled her throat, and murmured, "I think this is perfect timing. There's something I should tell you, though."

"It can't possibly beat 'I'm a wolf.'" Mabs tipped her chin so she could kiss his hair as she slid her fingers through it, and smiled when he met her eyes.

"No, but it's related to it."

"We'll have a litter if we decide to have kids some-day? No, you're an only child, that's probably not it." She laughed at Jake's eyes widened, and kissed him, softly at first, then with increasing intensity that made it clear the only thing keeping her from getting laid on the porch swing was the distinct possibility of Noah losing interest in the phone and coming to see what the grown-ups were doing. "Sorry," she mumbled eventually, not at all apologetically. "What did you want to say?"

Jake took a moment to shake off what looked like a glaze of pleasure, obviously trying to remember what he'd meant to ask. "Oh. Do you believe in fate?"

"Oh." Happy as she was where she was, Mabs tilted her chin back to look up at the house, then around at the front yard. "Oh, I don't know, a year ago I'd have said absolutely not. But this place...I don't know. Maybe it's changed me. It feels like home. It feels like it was meant to be. You feel like you were meant to be."

He closed his eyes, sighing like she'd somehow given him a gift, and nodded. "I think we were. My wolf thinks so too. You're...my fate, Mabs."

"That sounds amazing." Whispered words, as she ducked her head to hide her face against his neck before a little wave of uncertainty hit her. "Really? Kid and all?"

"Kid and all." Jake gathered her in his arms, hugging her so gently, so tightly. "I'm all in for the package deal, Mabs."

She sat up, not even embarrassed to push tears off her cheeks, and first smiled, then grinned, then laughed, the last sound verging on frustration. "This would be an *excellent* time to go to bed together."

Jake gave a wonderful, funny grimace and buried his face in her neck in turn. "It really would be," he mumbled. "I don't suppose we can convince Noah to go to bed early."

"It's four in the afternoon."

Jake laughed. "Yeah, okay, I didn't think so. What if I

made a really big dinner and filled him up so much he fell asleep?"

"You're welcome to try." Mabs suddenly squirmed, a wiggle of smug delight that ground her groin into Jake's and completely, *completely* distracted her from what she'd been going to say. He was so solid, in every imaginable way, and his hands clenched on her waist with sudden urgency.

A couple of gasping minutes later, Jake wheezed, "Damn, woman, I'm not gonna be able to walk to the kitchen if you do that again."

"Maybe I should..." Mabs fumbled her phone out of her hip pocket and found the name she wanted to call, then locked her gaze on Jake's as she spoke into the phone. "Sarah? Hey, um, yeah, hi, this is Ma...yeah, I know you know that. I was, uh, I was wondering if you could, like, emergency babysit Noah tonight?"

"Oh my God." Sarah's concern filled the line. "Of course I can. Is everything okay? Are you all right?"

"Oh, I'm good." Mabs thought her voice sounded hoarse, but she couldn't drag it back to normal.

All the worry drained out of Sarah's voice into delighted suspicion. "*How* good are you?"

Mabs swallowed, still looking into Jake's eyes. "*So* good."

Sarah actually cackled and Mabs thought she could hear her kicking her feet. "Yes! Yes! Yes! You're finally hooking up with Jake, aren't you? Whatever you're doing, keep doing it, I'll be there in twenty minutes and be out of there like a flash."

She hung up. Mabs put the phone away, biting her

lower lip with nervous hope, and said, "Think we can entertain ourselves for twenty minutes?"

Jake's voice dropped into a rumble. "I'm sure of it."

SARAH, true to her word, got there in just over twenty minutes, and somehow got Noah and his stuff out of the house in less than five, almost without making it necessary for Mabs to get out of Jake's lap. Left to her own devices, in fact, Sarah probably would have made sure Mabs *didn't* get out of Jake's lap, but as hot and sexy as Jake was, as horny as Mabs was, she also wasn't actually going to let her kid go spend the night somewhere else without saying goodbye.

Noah, by all appearances, didn't particularly care, planning, as he was, for pizza and "cheesy garlic bread without the cheese, Auntie Sarah." He hugged Mabs and promised to be good, then ran off to Sarah's truck with a teddy bear under his arm as Mabs stood on the porch and waved.

"Oh, God, he hasn't spent the night somewhere else before, I'm gonna get all sentimental and cry," she croaked as they drove away.

Jake stepped up behind her, sliding his arms around her and lowering his mouth to her shoulder to ask, "Should I distract you?"

Through a sniffle, she said, "I dunno if I can be-e-e- *oh*, oh, uh, uhm, yeah, okay," as he slipped a big hand down her tummy to curl it against her crotch. Breathless, she said, "Yeah, okay, go for it," and she felt his grin against her shoulder as, permission granted, he unbuttoned her jeans right there on the porch and slipped his hand back down, inside her underwear.

Mabs's knees buckled and he caught her with no effort at all, his fingers swirling in mind-numblingly pleasurable circles. Mabs said, "Oh my God," in a feeble voice, and reached up to clutch at the back of his neck, just trying to stay more or less upright. His breath came in short hot bursts against her throat, nonsense words of delight murmured there as she became increasingly incoherent.

Finally—although it really wasn't that long at all—she whimpered and tugged at his hand, trying half-heartedly to stop him. "Don't—? I'm gonna—I want to with you...."

"Yeah?"

At her nod, Jake slid his hand out of her pants, making her groan with dismay even if she'd asked for just that, turned her, and picked her up wholesale to walk into the house with her legs wrapped around his hips. Mabs said, "Oh my God," again, this time with gasping anticipation. "You're so big."

He walked her into the inside wall, pinning her, mumbled, "That's what she said," against her mouth, and laughed when she bit his lip, not very hard. "I deserved that."

"You did." She swallowed. "But she wasn't wrong, though. Put me down, put me..." His eyebrows went up in surprise, but he did as she asked, and, released from the complication of trying to get clothes off while wrapped around somebody, she shoved her jeans down, then kicked them off while pulling at his belt.

Jake drew a shuddering breath, catching her hands and stilling them for a moment. "Mabs, are you sure? This went from kind of zero to sixty pretty fast."

She blinked up at him, then smiled and drew him down for a kiss, finally mumbling, "I'm so sure. Thank you for asking. Are you—are *you* sure?"

"So sure," he echoed, then fumbled for his back pocket as Mabs decisively finished undoing his belt and fly. "Hang on, hang on, I gotta get a..."

"Oh, oh yeah, good idea." Mabs tried to kiss him again, totally hindering his efforts to get a condom out of his wallet, then giggled against his mouth. "Wait, I just have to check, you haven't been carrying that around since high school, right?"

Jake inched back enough to put on a wonderful expression of mock offense. "I have *not*." After exactly long enough to be funny, he added, "College, now..." and she burst out laughing while he paused to put the dang thing on. Half a second later he picked her up again, pinning her against the wall, and whispered, "Mabs," as he claimed her with a single glorious motion.

She cried out in pleasure, curling her arms around him as he slid his hands under her ass, holding her firmly in place. He felt perfect inside her, and within a few thrusts she was back where she'd been on the porch, on the very edge, and gasped, "Jake, I'm gonna—"

He whispered, "Yeah," against her mouth, and a few

seconds later waves of orgasm rolled through her, body-wracking shudders that left her sobbing with release and joy. Jake rumbled a sound of pleasure, just pressing into her until the deepest trembles began to ease. Then with slow, generous patience, brought her up again until suddenly he said, "Mabs," and buried himself in her even more deeply, triggering her own release again as his rocked through him. She gasped again, and laughed, and clung to him, and a very, *very* long time later, she finally mumbled a sated, "*Some* of us can't sleep comfortably on the floor, wolf-man," and led him up to bed.

CHAPTER 20

Jake woke to the scent of Mabs's lilac hair and a greater sense of contentment than he could ever remember. His wolf, unbearably smug, gave him a toothy grin, and he chuckled, drawing Mabs closer. She made a happy little sound and snuggled against him, then chuckled sleepily and slid her hand back, over his hip. "*Somebody's* awake."

"I already have a wolf living in my head," Jake murmured against her shoulder. "I don't need a personified penis, too. We can go with some *thing*, there."

Mabs laughed and rolled over to face him, hooking her leg over his hip instead. "Now that you've actually said that out loud, it seems like a much better choice. Hi."

"Hi." He slid his hand to the small of her back, pulling her closer yet, and bumped his nose against hers, dropping his voice. Not that they'd been talking loudly to begin with, but still. "How are you?"

She gave him a lazy smile. "Oh, I'm good."

Jake couldn't help smiling in return. "You *are*. Very good. But I mean...how are you?"

"Oh." Her smile, which was pretty soft to begin with, softened further, and she rolled back a bit, chin tipped up as she consulted the backs of her eyelids. Her throat, all long and lovely and stretched, wanted kisses, but Jake held off a moment, needing her answer first.

After a moment she tipped her head back down, meeting his eyes. "I'm good," she said again, this time more seriously, although the smile hadn't left her face. "I know it's maybe awkward to say so, maybe, but I do kind of want to jump up and text Sarah and see if she and Noah both survived the night. But I'm good. I'm really good. I'm happy." Her eyebrows rose. "I bet I'm also gonna be too sore to walk. It's been a *long* time."

Jake laughed and pulled her into a hug. "I'll carry you around all day if I have to."

"Oh, God, wouldn't Sarah just love that. No, I'll manage." Mabs buried her nose against his neck, sighing happily before she mumbled, "Thanks for asking. How, um, how are you?"

He grinned against her hair. "Really good. Probably not gonna be sore."

"How totally unfair. I guess that's what I get for slinging diner hash while you're lifting roof timbers. I need more ab workouts."

"I'm happy to provide them." Jake smiled again as she laughed, then nudged her a little. "Go text Sarah. I'll still be here. Or maybe in the kitchen cooking you some breakfast."

Mabs, sitting up, paused to stare at him in mild

dismay. "Now how am I supposed to choose between those two options? Oh, God, my tummy." She put a hand over her stomach and laughed. "Sore. Sore sore sore. Ow. Okay. Going to find my phone now. Ow ow ow." She crawled out of bed, pulling on a light silky robe that was almost as tantalizing as naked skin, and slid slippers on before she left the room.

Jake, having watched her every step of the way, admiring the view the whole time, fell back onto the bed and grinned like a fool at the ceiling.

Toldja, said his wolf, smugly.

"Yeah," Jake said aloud, if softly. "Yeah, you did. Thanks." Then, still smiling, he got up and went to make Mabs some breakfast.

ACCORDING TO MABS, neither Sarah nor Noah was dead, and she wasn't going to bring him home for several hours yet, for which Jake was eternally grateful. In the meantime, he and Mabs had breakfast, and then some more of what she euphemistically referred to as 'alone time,' and a shower which turned in to some more of that amazing 'alone time,' and they were both actually dressed and working on the house by the time Sarah showed up with Noah, sometime after noon.

It was snowing again by then, less hard than a few days before, but enough to suggest that winter had really truly arrived, weeks early. Noah was full of stories about spending the night at Sarah's, most of which Sarah corroborated. The little boy was clingier than usual, too, so Jake stepped back a bit, and, with Sarah's assistance, focused on getting plywood on the roof and letting Mabs and her son have their time.

When Noah had had enough Mommy Time and taken Wolf out to play in the snow, Jake came down from the roof to find Mabs in the kitchen. "We're off the roof and Sarah's having a snowball fight with Noah in the back yard. I'm sorry I can't do better by the roof right now. I'll get it sealed up enough to be warm, but I think we'd better take everything out of the attic, at least. And maybe out of the parlor-side bedrooms."

To his surprise, Mabs got up from peeling carrots and curled herself into his arms for a hard hug. "Thank you."

"You're welcome. Um, for what?"

"For not minding that Noah needed some Mommy Time. Or that I needed some Noah Time, for that matter."

"You said he's never spent the night away from you before," Jake said, still surprised. "I figured you'd want to spend time together. Why would I mind?"

"Because men can be really weird about women with kids? Anyway, thank you. I appreciate it." She smiled at him, and Jake's heart ached with the desire to just take care of her.

And it looked like he was going to be allowed to, which was the most incredible, amazing thing he'd ever imagined. "Whatever you need, Mabs," he said quietly. "I just want to be here for you. For both of you. I didn't come back to Virtue expecting to find everything I ever wanted, but I have."

Her smile got even brighter. "I didn't come to Virtue expecting anything but a roof over my head. *That's* gone kind of sideways, but boy, everything else is coming up roses."

"Hey! You have most of a roof over your head!"

Mabs laughed and stood on her toes to kiss him. "I know. And I'll have all of one again, come summer. Until then, I guess the buttery wing has a new roof so we can move everything in the bedrooms and attic into it? Because carrying a billion boxes of who-knows-what across half an acre of house sounds like such fun?"

"Everything sounds fun if it's with you," Jake promised, then laughed aloud at Mabs's skeptical expression. "Okay, that was cheesy."

"More than cheesy, it was wildly untrue. Jackassing boxes for days on end is nobody's idea of fun, even if it is with the love of your life."

Jake's heart contracted so hard his wolf became concerned. "Is that what I am?" he asked, almost breathlessly.

Mabs, squinting like she was trying to fight off a smile, looked him up and down and lost the fight with the smile. "You know what? I think you are. Is that okay?"

He picked her up, earning a squeak, and spun her around the kitchen. "It's amazing, because I know you're the love of mine."

"Because your wolf told you so?"

"Because I never wanted to leave your side from the moment I first walked into this kitchen and saw you." Jake set Mabs back on her feet and smiled down at her.

Her own smile, already wide, broadened further. "You know Sarah's going to be unbearably smug for all time, right?"

"So's my wolf," he promised. "So I guess we're okay."

"Great." Mabs stepped out of his arms, turned him away from her, and gave him a smack on the butt. "Then let's go move some boxes."

Jake gave a perfunctory yelp and headed for the door. "I suddenly begin to suspect you do not have a romantic soul, Mary Anne Brannigan."

"You think a woman who moves to a broken-down farm house in upstate New York, hires a carpenter for the price of a barn room, and falls in love with him, doesn't have a romantic soul?" She followed him, and when he glanced over his shoulder, made no apology for having clearly been checking out his backside.

A zing of desire shot through him and he grinned. "I guess if you put it that way...."

"I do. Now scoot, we got work to do."

"Yes, ma'am."

SARAH VOLUNTEERED to watch Noah for a while, since it was clear emptying the attic would take a lot of adult attention. The afternoon flew by with Mabs mostly in the attic, lugging boxes and whatever furniture she could lift to the little door in the floor and handing them down to Jake, who went up and down the ladder more times than he could count. Sarah stacked boxes on the landing and kept Noah from rummaging through them, which Mabs said was the harder job. Jake went up for the heaviest stuff himself, the women shouting and swearing as they balanced it when he handed it down, and Noah, in the background, scolding everybody for their language.

But before dinner, they'd cleared the attic out, and Sarah, staying for leftover turkey, got to have Thanksgiving dinner with them after all. Mabs, dramatically throwing herself into a kitchen chair after dinner, said, "They can stay on the landing for tonight. We'll move them to the buttery wing tomorrow, and start on the bedrooms after that. Sarah, I owe you..." She waved a tired hand in the air. "I don't even know."

"A million massages," Sarah suggested.

Mabs lit up, straightening in her chair. "I'm supposed to practice on volunteers, so yeah! That's a great idea!"

"I volunteer as tribute!" Sarah put on an expression of self-sacrifice that made everybody, even Noah, laugh.

He ran around the kitchen shouting, "I volunteer as tribute!" until Mabs picked him up, said, "As tribute for a BATH?" and hauled him upstairs, protesting, to be washed. Mabs yelled, "G'bye if you leave before I come back down!" at Sarah, who got up for another piece of pie.

"Are you kidding, I'm never leaving. Jake?"

"I'm never leaving either."

Sarah gave him a sly, but pleased, smile. "You two

really hit it off, huh? I'm glad. I really am. She's great, and you were always nice. Now do you want pie or not?"

"I'll make some more whipped cream." Jake got up to do so, and for a minute the whir of the mixer drowned out conversation. When the cream was done, though, he said, "Thanks for introducing us. I didn't mean to stay in Virtue at all, but I kinda think I'm gonna."

"Oh, you think?" Sarah handed Jake a piece of pie and he blopped whipped cream on it, then lifted his eyebrows to see if she wanted some. She extended her plate and he put a big scoop of cream on her pie, too, then sat down at the table as she said, "I'm glad, though. I guess half our graduating class is still here, but they're not necessarily the ones I'd have chosen to stay. I'd have chosen you to."

Jake, around a mouthful of pie, said, "I'm flattered," and actually meant it.

"Well, you're the only one who could restore all the old houses the historical society wants work done on, so maybe don't read too much into it." She winked and Jake laughed.

"Gee, thanks." His wolf muttered, sulking, and Jake laughed again, both at Sarah and the wolf.

Sarah smiled, finished her pie, and stood. "I'm going home before Mabs finds another job for me to do."

"Wise choice. There's a never-ending list of things to do around here."

"Yeah. I can tell you're suffering." Sarah grabbed her things, yelled, "Bye Mabs! Bye Noah!" up the stairs, and was nearly out the door before a soap-bubbly, naked four-year-old came running down the stairs to slam into her legs for a hug. Mabs, drenched from collarbone to mid-thigh—which would have been alluring if it weren't for her grim expression, and maybe was anyway—thudded down the stairs after him and struggled to grab his soap-slick-self and carry him back to the tub.

"It's like wrestling a greased pig," she said in despair as they disappeared up the stairs again.

Sarah leaned on the door and wiped tears of laughter from her eyes. "Look what you've gotten yourself into, Jacob Timothy Rowly."

Jake grinned after Mabs and Noah, then at Sarah. "Yeah," he said happily. "Isn't it great?"

CHAPTER 21

There were about seventy 'best things' that Mabs could think of regarding having a new boyfriend, but a warm snuggly body in bed with her was at the top of that list the next morning. Or it was, at least, until she had to get out of the cozy bed. Jake made a lazy grab to pull her back, missed, pouted, and sent Mabs to the shower with a dippy little smile firmly in place. There was a giant hole plywood-ed over in her roof, and an ex to deal with, and she'd absolutely never been happier in her life. Jake kissed her goodbye on her way to work, promising he'd get some of the boxes moved down to the buttery wing, and she went off with Noah in tow.

She thought the work day might drag, keeping her away from Jake as it did, but a little to her surprise, it flew by, people in and out of the diner all day to talk about the unseasonable snow, shopping for the holidays, and whatever bits of family gossip had been generated over the long weekend. Mabs was exhausted at the end of the day, but felt absurdly light and happy anyway, eager to go home to Jake and get more work on the house done.

He'd gotten all the boxes moved from the landing, and with Noah's 'assistance' they cleared out the smallest of the parlor-side front bedrooms before Mabs declared it more than enough work for one day. She was even more reluctant to go to work the next morning, but did anyway, and as the lunch rush slowed, Judge Owens came in with a perplexed frown. "Can I talk to you for a minute, Mabs?"

Mabs cast a glance at her boss, who waved her off, and followed the judge outside into a cloudy afternoon. "Smells like snow," the judge said, still frowning. "Who's Brent Mitchell, Mabs?"

"I didn't know snow had a sm...ugh." Mabs's heart rate shot up and she took a deep breath, wrapping her arms around herself. "He's my ex-boyfriend. Noah's biological father. Did he lawyer up like he said he was going to?"

Faint lines of disapproval formed around the judge's mouth. "He seems to think he doesn't need a lawyer, and is asking for a child custody hearing as soon as possible. Are you working Friday afternoon?"

"Until three, but I can ask Russ to let me off earlier if you need." Mabs's hands went cold with nervousness, even as she reminded herself that Jake would be there to support her.

"I can make 3:30 work, if you can get to the courthouse by then." At Mabs's nod, Judge Owens said, "Good. I'll get the letters notifying you of the court date in the mail this afternoon and I'll see you on Friday."

Mabs said, "Thank you," faintly. "Isn't this a little...informal, Judge?"

Judge Owens's eyebrows rose. "He's filed, I'm sending a letter of notification, it's all on the books. Can I help it if I know most of the people in my jurisdiction by name and find it easier to drop by their workplace to make sure a day is convenient for them, rather than doing it all by letter and phone?"

A smile crept over Mabs's face. "I guess not. Thank you, Judge."

"Sure thing." The judge went to her car, cracking the door open before she glanced up again. "Mabs? What on earth was he talking about a wolf for?"

Mabs's gut clenched before she let out a wheezy laugh. "I'll explain on Friday."

"Good. I'll send the letter," Judge Owens promised, and got in her car to drive away.

INTELLECTUALLY, Mabs knew she had nothing to worry about. Brent was the very definition of a deadbeat dad. Noah had never even *met* him, except the once when he'd shown up at Mabs's house while Jake was babysitting. He hadn't supported them financially, or been any part of their lives. Intellectually, she knew all that.

It didn't help at all, emotionally. She got through the rest of the work day and went home with Noah, trying to keep an everything's-all-right facade up. It worked on the four-year-old, but Jake's expression darkened to worry as soon as she came in the door. "I can't talk about it right now," she told him quietly, and all he did was draw her into a reassuring hug, instead of nagging her to tell him.

Mabs could have cried just for that little kindness, but he washed up from doing construction work and made dinner too, while she played with Noah and tried to get her state of mind straightened out. She felt better by the time Jake served up a stew with homemade biscuits, and considerably better after she'd eaten four of them with blackberry jam from the Halloween festival.

All of that restored equilibrium was wrecked by Noah fighting about bedtime for nearly two hours. Mabs staggered back downstairs, not even actually triumphant, at nearly her *own* bedtime. Jake was at the kitchen table with a book, a cup of coffee, and a new pair of reading glasses that for some reason made her entire body and soul go directly into horny overdrive. Even exhausted and angry at her kid, it worked well enough to restore some of her sense of humor. She sat down, put her head on the table, and muttered, "Maybe I should *let* him take him."

Jake took his reading glasses off and put them on the table. "I don't think that would make you happy, in the end."

"No," she mumbled. "I guess not. I've put an awful lot of work into him at this point. I'd hate for Brent to screw it all up." She turned her head so she could see him better. "Judge Owens asked if I could come for a court date on Friday. Custody case, I guess. I don't even know if that's what it is, if there hasn't been a drawn-out legal battle around it."

Jake rose, came to move the chair beside her, and crouched in that space, putting his hand over hers on the table. "What do you need me to do?"

Mabs made a sound somewhere between a laugh and a sob, and slid off the chair into his arms. "I think I need you to just keep being you. Nobody's ever asked me that before."

Jake's warm arms closed around her and he chuckled into her hair. "I can do that, but if there's anything more concrete, I can do that too."

"There is something. The appointment is at 3:30 at the courthouse, and I need you to bring something there for me. Can you do that?"

"Yeah, of course. Just tell me what." He kissed her hair, then tipped her chin up to kiss her lips, too. "It's going to be all right, Mabs."

Mabs nodded mutely and buried her face against Jake's shoulder. "I'm so tired," she finally said, and felt him smile against her hair.

"Probably because some brute has been keeping you up much later than you're used to."

A giggle escaped her. "Probably."

"Should the brute carry you up to bed? For sleeping?"

Mabs leaned back to look at him slightly incredulously. "On those stairs? Isn't that taking both our lives into your hands?"

"Maybe, but you're very small." Jake stood, offering Mabs a hand up.

"I'm not *very* small! I'm—I'm *pretty* small." She took his hand, standing, then yelped in delight as he scooped her into a bride's carry. "Okay, from your perspective maybe I'm very small."

"I'm happy to go with 'pretty.'" Jake kissed her, somehow managed to turn the kitchen light off while maneuvering them both through the door, and carried her upstairs without clobbering anybody's head or knee or shoulder. A few minutes later, teeth brushed, pajamas on, Mabs fell asleep nestled in his arms, which was as good an end to any day as she could imagine.

THE VIRTUE COURTROOM matched Mabs's idea of what a small town courtroom *should* look like, with a wood-paneled interior and high windows with small panes in them. It was less intimidating than she expected, even if her heart was still beating too hard as she'd entered the lobby with Noah. Jake had been waiting for her, as promised, and said, "I'll keep an eye on him," even though they'd already agreed he would.

There was a bailiff and a court stenographer, but the only other person in the room just then was the judge, who looked pleased at Mabs's arrival. "You're a few minutes early, Ms. Brannigan. Mr. Mitchell isn't here yet. I don't like having children in the courtroom when their parents are discussing custody, but if you wouldn't mind, I'd like to talk to Noah alone for a few minutes?"

"Sure." Mabs's voice cracked with nerves. "He's in the lobby with Jake. Should I go get him?"

"I'll go out to talk to him." The judge rose in a swoop of black robes and went out like she owned the place, which Mabs guessed she kind of did. She sat, waiting, and Brent, dressed in a suit and with his hair freshly cut, came in before the judge returned. Mabs nodded at him, but realized she really had nothing to say, so just...didn't. It felt refreshing, and it obviously annoyed Brent, which was an unexpected bonus.

Judge Owens returned at exactly 3:30 and listened to Brent's impassioned speech about family values and how he'd grown as a person and the effort it had taken to find Mabs and Noah. Mabs moved restlessly in her seat, wondering again *how* he'd found them, but it didn't seem like the time to ask. Finally his speech wound up and the judge, without changing expression, said, "The court would like to see your financial paperwork showing that you've paid child support for the past four years, please, Mr. Mitchell."

"My what?"

Mabs narrowly fought off a grin as a look of impatient expectation crossed the judge's face. "Your tax paperwork showing you've paid child support," she repeated. "Where is it?"

"Oh, I don't—have it."

"And why is that?"

"Uh, I, uh, uh."

"Ms. Brannigan, do you have any insight as to where this paperwork might be?"

"I'd be surprised if there is any, Judge. I've never received any child support from him."

"What does that matter?" Brent demanded. "She's living in an unfit house with my son—"

Judge Owens did not have a drawl. She drawled, "Well, now, I've been in that house myself, Mr. Mitchell, and it wasn't even unfit when I was last there, three months ago. Given that it's been under constant restoration since then, I can't imagine it's unfit now."

"There's a hole in the roof!"

The judge looked inquiringly at Mabs, who spread her hands a little. "That early snow broke the roof's support beam, but it's in the half of the house we're not living in yet. It's plywooded over now, and the attic is Visqueened off for warmth and safety. I have pictures, if you'd like to see."

"I've seen them," the judge said, almost cheerfully. "They went around on the historical society's WhatsApp group. The court is satisfied with the condition of your home."

"What about the *wolf*?" Brent's voice broke, and Judge Owens's expression became even more enquiring as she looked to Mabs again.

"If I can open the courtroom door for a minute, please, Judge?"

The judge's eyebrows lifted with interest and she nodded. Mabs went to the door and Jake handed her the thing she'd asked him to bring for her. She came back in holding Noah's puppy under his front legs, which was harder now than it had been three months earlier. "This is Wolf, Judge Owens."

"Get that damn dog away from me!" Brent rose and backed up several feet, fury contorting his face. "That's a *dog*. I saw a *wolf*."

Somehow the judge managed to convey the impression of looking over the top edge of glasses, even though she wasn't wearing them, as Brent scrambled as far away from Mabs and the puppy as he could get. "You don't like dogs, Mr. Mitchell?"

"That's not a crime!"

"Not at all. Ms. Brannigan, if you could bring Wolf back out into the hall? He appears to be causing the plaintiff some distress."

"Of course, Judge." Mabs handed the puppy back to Jake, who winked as the doors closed between them again.

Judge Owens's expression became serious as Mabs returned to her place in the courtroom. "As I'm sure both of you know, the legal system is reluctant to deny all access to a child to biological parents." Mabs's heart sank, and a nasty smile ran across Brent's face, although as the judge continued, his smile faded and Mabs's heart rose.

"That said, the legal system also likes to see parental involvement in a child's life. Ms. Brannigan has testified here that Mr. Mitchell has had no involvement, financial or otherwise, in the child's life. Furthermore, upon questioning, the child himself was unable to identify Mr. Mitchell as anything other than 'the mean man that Mr. 'Growly' scared off.' Mr.

'Growly', for the record, is known to the court as Jacob Rowly."

Brent howled, "A *wolf* scared me off! I don't know any Jacob Rowly!"

The judge gave Brent an utterly scathing look. "Are you suggesting to the court that Jacob Rowly is a wolf, Mr. Mitchell?"

Mabs's breath seized, but ugly color rose along Brent's jaw and curdled his cheeks. "That would be stupid."

"Well then," Judge Owens said, as if he'd settled the matter. "Mr. Mitchell, in your limited exposure to the child in question, your behavior has been threatening and aggressive. You have provided no evidence of support, and your arguments in favor of an unfit environment have been found wanting.

"Your petition is denied. I see no reason to allow you any rights, visitation or otherwise, to a child you have shown no interest in. If your child wishes to engage with you in the future, this court is willing to concede that that is their right, but you will not, under penalty of law, initiate contact with either Noah or Mary Anne Brannigan. Is my ruling clear?"

Brent made an inarticulate sound of rage that prompted Judge Owens to nod at the bailiff, who stepped forward with the air of a man eager to do his job. Brent, flushed with fury, stalked out with the bailiff trailing him to the door. Mabs whispered, "Thank you, Judge Owens," and the judge crooked a finger, beckoning her to the bench.

When she approached, the judge leaned forward,

hands clasped together. "An advantage to being a small-town judge is knowing who you're dealing with, but I wouldn't be surprised if that man puts in an appeal to a higher court. You should be prepared for that. But more importantly, I need you to listen to me very carefully right now."

Mabs, quaking, gave a mute nod to indicate she was listening, and Judge Owens exhaled a mighty sigh. "I'm glad he was there to help you, Mabs, but tell Jake Rowly to be more careful, in the future."

abs came out of the court room so white that if Jake hadn't seen Brent Mitchell stomp off in a fury, he would have thought she'd lost the court case. He picked up Wolf's carrying kennel and put an arm around her waist, offering support while he murmured, "Are you all right?"

She took Noah's hand as they left the courthouse, shaking her head, and whispered, "I'll tell you later."

"All right. All right." He kissed her hair, trying not to worry. His wolf, its fur fluffed up with concern, said, *We should have bitten him*, and Jake fought off the urge to shift, chase Brent Mitchell down, and do just that.

"Is that mean man gone now?" Noah asked, distracting him.

Mabs's smile suddenly blossomed. "He is, baby. The judge told him he wasn't allowed to come back."

Noah beamed. "Does that mean Mr. Growly is my daddy now?"

Jake's heart lurched so hard he missed a step.

Nothing sounded better to him, but he would never have dared to say it so bluntly, or so early in their relationship. He was almost afraid to look at Mabs, sure that she wouldn't be ready to even think about something so permanent, or so...so life-changing. So *real*, especially in how it affected Noah.

To his relief, and delight, and joy, she shot him a sparkling smile, then picked Noah up. "Mr. Growly and I aren't quite ready to talk about that yet, baby. Do you think that would be a good idea, though?"

Noah nodded emphatically and Mabs, kissing him on the cheek, said, "I'll keep that in mind, then."

"Okay. Can we have pizza?"

"Yeah. I think going out for pizza sounds like a great idea, sweetheart." She put Noah down again and he ran to her car, climbing into his safety seat and waiting for the slow adults to catch up.

Jake slowed down a little more, though. "Mabs, is everything okay? You looked like you'd seen a ghost when you came out."

Mabs blurted, "Judge Owens knows you're a shapeshifter and says to be more careful."

"She..." Jake felt his jaw drop and reeled it back up with effort. "Are you sure?"

"Yeah. Yeah, I'm sure." Mabs's eyes were wide and worried.

Jake shook his head, baffled. "Nobody knows, nob...we don't ta...how ca...hang on." He pulled his phone out, eyebrows drawn down so hard he was getting a headache, and called his parents.

His mom picked up after three or four rings, her cheerful, "Hello, this is Rhonda," coming down the line.

"Hi, Mom, it's Jake."

"Oh! Jake! Hi, honey! How are you? I haven't talked to you in months."

"I know, I'm sorry." Jake made a face at Mabs, who could obviously overhear at least some of what his mom was saying. She smiled, tilted her head toward the car, and went to keep an eye on Noah as he trailed along behind, saying, "I've been busy. I, uh. I'm back in Virtue, actually."

His mom's voice went dry. "Dumped you, did she? Dammit, I knew we should have kept the ho—Mark! I *told* you we should have kept the house, Jake is back in Virtue! That twit he was seeing dumped him! Hold on," she said, back to Jake. "Your father is picking up another phone."

Almost before she'd finished speaking, his dad picked up and said, "She was never the right one for you anyway, son. You'll know, when you meet your mate."

"Yeah, well, about that—I mean, no, I mean, *yes*, but look, I'm back in Virtue and old Ms. Brannigan died—"

His parents both said, "Oh, no," in perfunctory tones that made Jake smile.

"—and her grand-niece or something, she inherited the place and I've been fixing it up for her, and—"

"Oooh." His mother sounded delighted. "Is she pretty?"

Jake, completely derailed said, "Oh my God, Mom,

she's amazing," and he could nearly hear both his parents kicking their feet with delight.

"Is she the one, Jake? Did your wolf let you know?" His dad sounded hopeful. "Are you getting married?"

"Yeah, I think she—yeah, it di—no! No! She's got a four-year-old, we're not moving that fa—that's not the point! Dad! Mom! Stop!"

"Well, if you'd call more often we wouldn't have to grill you when you do," his mom said. "When do we get to meet her? Does she know about the wolf?"

"I don't know! Yes! She was amazing about it. Mom! Stop! Does Judge Owens know about *us* ?"

"Vicky? Victoria Owens? How is she, I haven't talked to her in years. Are her kids all out of school yet?"

"Uh, no, she's got one more who's a junior or a senior, Mom, does she know about us?"

"I assume she must, or you wouldn't be asking, but she's not from a shifter family, honey. But you know Virtue." His mom's shrug was almost audible over the phone. "Everybody knows everybody's business and has for over two hundred years. Honestly all the old-school shifter politics is part of why your father and I decided to move out west. There's a really nice pack out here in Silver Springs, just very casual, none of that trying to keep the ancient pure bloodlines going thing, it's much more stable than that."

"We were going to suggest you come out here when you eventually broke up with that woman," his dad said. "But you didn't *tell* us you'd broken up."

"And that's turned out just fine, hasn't it," his mom said, obviously no longer talking to Jake. "Really, Mark, you don't have to micromanage his whole life—"

"Well, how could I, he left home before his mortarboard hit the ground after graduation! He's turned out fine, the carpentry thing worked—"

"Even though you were skeptical—"

"Yes, fine, even though I was skeptical, and it sounds like he's *finally* found his mate—"

"Look, Mark, not everybody is lucky enough to find what they're looking for in their own home town, and isn't that part of why we left Virt—"

Jake, grinning, said, "I have to go get dinner now. I love you guys. I'll call again soon," and hung up with no doubt that they would continue their low-key argument, probably still on the phone. Mabs and Noah were waiting in the car, and Mabs rolled the window down as he approached. "Mom says she never told the judge anything, but she wouldn't be surprised if she knows because the Owens are old Virtue families. I'll meet you at the pizza place?"

"Okay. As long as you're safe." Mabs pulled him down for a quick kiss, then nodded. "See you there."

MABS AND JAKE ate enough to stuff themselves, but Noah somehow managed to put away an entire 9-inch mozzarella pizza entirely on his own. Mabs insisted they all take a walk along the river after dinner in order to keep him awake long enough to make it to bedtime. Wolf, who'd been cooped up in the carrying kennel in the back of Jake's truck while they ate, was delighted, and both boy and puppy were barely conscious with exhaustion by the time they got home. Mabs got Noah tucked into bed, then came downstairs and simply crawled into Jake's lap.

He curled his arms around her, overwhelmed with the urge to protect her. "You doing all right?"

"I actually am," she replied, muffled. "Emotionally wrung out, I think, but actually okay. The judge ruling in my favor obviously helped, but then I thought I was gonna have a heart attack when she wanted to warn you to be careful. It never occurred to me there might be people around here who knew. Does Sarah?"

"I don't think so, but I wouldn't have thought Judge Owens did either. Sarah's family hasn't been in Virtue as long, though. I think her great-grandparents came here after the Civil War."

"Oh," Mabs said, still muffled. "So only *most* of two hundred years, instead of *more* than two hundred years. Sure, I can totally see how that would lead to them not knowing the town secrets."

"Okay, when you put it that way...."

Mabs lifted her head, smiling. "Yeah. That's what I thought. Did you have, uh, like, other shapeshifter friends to play with, growing up?"

"A few. Most of them have left Virtue, too, though. It's kinda gotten that way the past few generations, unless you want to marry your cousin or something. Especially for shifters."

"I guess a lot of small towns are like that, though. Even if they're not full of shapeshifters." Mabs leaned her head against his shoulder, eyes closed, and sat for a while without saying anything. Jake stole a couple of kisses that made her smile, and she finally murmured, "There's a huge amount of work to do tomorrow, so obviously going to bed really early tonight is the right thing to do, right?"

"I'll never say no to that proposition," Jake promised, but lifted his eyebrows. "What work?"

She gave him a skeptical look from up close. "Emptying out all the parlor-side bedrooms so we can just totally weatherproof that side of the house and forget about it until spring?"

Jake groaned, although he didn't really mean it. "Oh yeah. That work. Are you sure we can't just stay in bed all weekend?"

"Even if I wanted to, and I confess I would love to, I've noticed that no matter how late I go to bed, my child still gets up at the same time and expects me to be available to cater to most of his needs. So...yeah, I'm afraid I'm pretty sure staying in bed all weekend isn't an option. At least, not for me. I guess you could."

"What fun would that be if you weren't there?" Jake stole another kiss, this one meandering toward meaning business, until finally he scooped her up. "To bed with us."

Mabs yelped and laughed. "I could get used to you carrying me around."

"Anywhere you want," Jake promised, and thought, but didn't say, *including across the threshold.*

She'd say yes, his wolf opined.

I'll wait until I'm sure, Jake replied, and carried Mabs up to bed.

*N*oah, having gone to bed early, was up early, too, and Mabs woke to a shrieking child and a barking puppy. She left Jake to sleep a while—although how he could sleep through the commotion, she didn't know—and made pancakes for breakfast before dressing and going upstairs to let herself into Aunt Doris's old bedroom. Noah came in to help for a while, but lost interest in boxes of old photographs, bags of knitting projects, and stacks of diaries much more quickly than Mabs herself ever would.

She didn't have time to go through the photos then, but she carried them downstairs to the buttery itself, rather than the rooms behind it, so she could look at them later. The knitting supplies she put into thrift shop bags, because while the idea of learning to knit sounded wonderful, Mabs knew herself well enough to suspect it would just go down in a long list of things she could beat herself up for not actually doing. *Not* beating herself up seemed like a better idea, so the supplies would be happier with someone else who would use them.

"Great," she muttered to herself on the way back up to Doris's bedroom, "now I think yarn and knitting needles have *feelings*. I need to get out more."

She genuinely wanted to read the diaries, so they came off the bedside table and shelves and went into a box she brought to the living room that they'd made from what would normally be a dining room area. Next summer, Mabs promised herself. Next summer, once the parlor was restored and turned into a living room, she would return the dining room to its original state and invite people over for dinner. But that was for next year, and for now, she was happy to have a snuggly little warm living room behind the kitchen. She put the box of diaries on the coffee table and went back to pack up—or throw out—everything else in the room.

The stack of stuff for the thrift shop was taller than she was, before she had finished. Jake had appeared while she worked, distracting her with kisses that came dangerously close to more before Noah, out in the yard, yelled about something and reminded them both of just who might interrupt them. Jake let her go reluctantly, murmuring, "Do you need any help in here?"

"Not yet. I want to clear the bed out, but I'm going to do that last. I've found a bunch of places in here already where snow dripped through, so we might think about getting insulation between the attic floor boards and the ceiling in here soon, but not until it's empty."

"Probably a good idea. Tell you what, I'll start on the other bedroom, but call me if you need help, okay?"

Mabs fluttered her eyelashes. "I will, you big strong handsome man."

Jake, laughing, left her to work, and between lunch and playing with Noah and work, she got the room pretty well empty by late afternoon. Jake—being bigger, stronger, and perhaps due to being handsome, but she doubted it—cleared out the larger of the two front bedrooms. He'd even applied winterization to the whole front half of the upstairs before going down to the living room to play with Noah. Mabs, sweaty and tired, staggered downstairs in Jake's wake a little while later and collapsed on the couch. "I'm never gonna move again."

"I'm cooking dinner then, eh?" Jake gave her a fond smile.

"I don't care. I don't think I can eat."

Noah, dismayed, howled, "*I* want to eat!", and Mabs grabbed him into a hug, nomming at his elbows and ears.

"You want to be eaten? You want to be eaten? Okay, I'll eat you!"

"Mommy! Mommy, no! I want to *eat*! I'm *hungry*!"

Jake, getting to his feet, asked, "Tuna melts sound good?"

"Ooh," Mabs said. "So good."

"What's a tuna melt?"

"Tuna fish on toast with melted cheese on top."

"I don't *like* cheese!"

"You ate an entire cheese pizza last night!"

Utter betrayal widened Noah's eyes. "That wasn't *cheese*. That was *mozzarella*!"

"Mozzarella," Mabs informed him, "is a kind of cheese. And I think we've got some shredded mozzarella in the fridge, so do you want a tuna-mozzarella-melt?"

"Yeeeeeeeeesssssss!" Noah leaped up and ran a victory lap around the living room, Wolf barking wildly at his heels.

Mabs made the best soulful puppy dog eyes at Jake that she could. "Tuna melts with mozzarella for one, and whatever kind of cheese you want for everybody else?"

Jake, grinning, bent to kiss her. "Your wish is my command, but you should know I'm genetically immune to puppy dog eyes."

"Aw, jeez, I guess you would be. Okay, fine. I'll just look adoringly at you." Mabs tried to look adoring and ended up laughing, but Jake went to make tuna melts anyway. Mabs pulled one of the diaries from the box and opened it to a random page from 1945.

She breathed, "Holy moly," and took another book out to discover it was from even earlier. She started putting them in chronological order, setting the most recent one beside her on the couch as she sorted the rest of them out, then gazed at the box in wonder. A whole lifetime's worth of diaries, chronicling nearly a century of experiences. The historical society was going to love them.

She had to wash her hands for dinner before she got to start reading, and then of course there was bath and bedtime, but, determined to get at least *some* diary-reading in, after Noah was in bed, Mabs curled onto the couch with the last of them.

Jake snuggled down beside her with a novel and his reading glasses, so she couldn't let herself even look at him or she'd get too horny to think. He did smell wonderful, though. That was distracting, but then the day to day minutia of Aunt Doris's life drew Mabs in. She read the pages slowly, finding them filled with how the modern world conflicted with how Doris used to run the old farm.

The old lady hadn't written daily—more like once or twice a week—so the diary covered a couple of years' worth of time. After a while, Mabs exhaled in surprise, murmuring, "Listen to this, she says, 'That annoying young man came by again, trying to get me to sell the place. You'd think Robert Cole's grandson would know better.' That was—" She checked the date — "Just over two years ago. It sounds like Preston has wanted this place for a long time."

"Developers are persistent bastards," Jake agreed. "I'm glad you decided not to sell."

"I'm glad *she* decided not to sell." Mabs went back to reading, and a few minutes later said, "Oh, listen, there's more. She says Jennifer Minor came by, that's the woman up the road who rents some of the acreage for her horses?"

"Yeah, I know Jen, we went to school together. Well, I went to school with her brother. She was a few years behind us, but we'd hang out sometimes. What about her?" Jake put his chin on top of Mabs's head, like he was trying to read through her.

"Preston was trying to get her to sell, too. Doris says the fact that she wouldn't gave Jennifer the resolve to hold her ground. She sounds proud of that. 'No sense in being 92 if you can't be stubborn for the young folks,' she says. What does he even want all this land for? They can't want to put an outlet mall in, there aren't even enough people in the area to support it. Did they find gold or oil beside the river or something?"

"Developers always think they can eke another few dollars out of the locals," Jake said with a shrug. "Maybe they want to turn Virtue into a sleeper community for Schenectady."

"Oh, come on, we're closer to Ottawa."

He grinned against her hair. "I didn't say it was a good guess." After a moment's silence, he said, "A resort is probably more likely, though, now that you make that point. Nobody's gonna drive two or three hours from Virtue to work, but they might drive up here for a week's vacation."

Mabs, thinking of the creek on the land, and the acres of forest and green, as well as the open fields, nodded. "Yeah, maybe it was a resort. They sent me paperwork ages go, right after I'd inherited the place. I threw it away without really looking at it, but that sounds familiar. Too bad, I'd have been willing to dig for some gold." She turned another page of the diary, her eyebrows drawing down as she read further. "He was really nagging her."

"Preston was never a great human being."

"Yeah, but no, I mean..." Mabs flipped ahead a few pages, frowning. "She mentions him more and more. She even talks about calling the sheriff."

Jake shifted behind her so he could actually look at the diary's pages. "Did she?"

"Not that she says, but..." Mabs fell silent again, rifling through the book. "But she got to where she was afraid of him and then—Jesus. And then I guess she died, because the entries stop. Well, that's horrible. God." She put the diary down and twisted to face Jake, her head starting to ache from the intensity of her frown. "I mean...you don't think he could have had anything to do with her death, do you?"

"She *was* 93," Jake said gently.

"Yeah, I know, but that's like—would you even think to look for any evidence of foul play if the victim was a 93 year old woman who lived on her own? They said she just died in her sleep, which you'd expect, right? But what if she didn't? But that's probably just...I don't know. Crazy talk."

"Maybe. Probably," Jake admitted. "I don't know how we'd tell, either, without exhuming her, and even then..."

Mabs shook her head. "She was cremated anyway, so that wouldn't help. I don't know. I might try talking to her doctor, or the sheriff, or...both..."

"Would it make you feel better?"

"It kind of would, yeah."

Jake leaned in to kiss her, murmuring, "Then it's what you should do. But not tonight," against her mouth. "It's too late for investigations tonight."

"I can think of some things I'd like to investigate."

"Yeah? Can they be investigated on the couch?"

"You know what, I think they can..." Mabs, gratefully, let questions about her great-aunt slip from her mind, and they finally went to bed much, much later.

MABS WAS UP EARLY the next morning, but then, she was always up early, since Noah considered 7:30 to be an unbearably late morning. She left Doris's bedroom alone for the time being, not wanting to try moving the mattress and bed frame out without Jake's help, and as soon as it was late enough, called the sheriff's office to see if Doris Brannigan had ever filed a complaint about Preston Cole.

"Not as such," the deputy told her thoughtfully. "She told the sheriff he was a nuisance, a couple of times when he saw her around town, but no formal complaints. How come?"

"I don't know," Mabs said unhappily. "I'm just wondering. And...there wasn't anything suspicious about her death?"

The deputy's voice sharpened. "Not that I'm aware of, no. Why do you ask?"

"I don't know," Mabs said again. "I'm sure it's nothing."

"But you're not," the deputy said, "or you wouldn't be asking these questions."

Mabs sighed. "Yeah. But I don't have any reason to be suspicious, except a twitchy feeling. I'm given to understand that gut feelings aren't actually basis for police work."

A little to her surprise, the deputy chuckled. "No, not really, but you let us know if anything more than a gut feeling comes to light, all right? Everybody around here liked Doris Brannigan. Nobody would want to imagine something worse than old age happened to her."

"I'll let you know." Mabs hung up the phone and went to deal with the pillows and quilts on Doris's old bed, at least. Noah came bouncing in after her and jumped on the bed, sending dust everywhere, and Mabs coughed, trying to brush it off him. He squirmed away, and she paused just before dusting her hands together, staring at the fine crumbs stuck to her palms. Holding her hands carefully open so she couldn't knock any of it off, she went to find Jake in the kitchen. "What is this?"

He turned her palm up, looking at the dust in the light. "Looks like sawdust."

"That's what I thought." Mabs wet her lips. "It was all over Doris's bed."

They both looked at the kitchen ceiling, as if it would hold answers. "It could've fallen through the slats in her ceiling," Jake said after a moment. "From the attic."

"I don't remember seeing sawdust up there. Of course, I was shoveling snow in the middle of the night."

"You know what," Jake said slowly, "I put the weather barrier up in the middle of the night, too, and I didn't take any of it down again when I was nailing the plywood in place. I haven't really looked at that broken beam up there. Maybe we should."

"Are we going into the haunted attic?" Noah appeared in the kitchen door, looking hopeful.

"Is the attic haunted?" Mabs asked, amused. "Jake and I are going up. You're not."

Unmitigated devastation rose in Noah's face. "But I want to see the ghosts!"

"Ghosts don't come out in the day," Mabs said absently. "But we'll need you and Wolf to protect the bottom of the ladder in case I'm wrong."

Sheer delight replaced Noah's dismay and he charged up the stairs, yelling, "I'm gonna get you, ghosts!"

Mabs and Jake, both smiling, followed him upstairs, and Jake pulled the attic ladder down. Mabs thought she could watch him do that forever, stretching all long and lean like that, but to her sorrow, the show ended as quickly as it had begun. She went up first, aware that even if she didn't get a good view that way, Jake did, as proven by his sound of appreciation as she climbed up in front of him.

He started moving plastic sheets out of the way as soon as they got up there, mostly directing her to hold something, or step over there, as her part of helping. Noah yelled, "No monsters yet!" from the foot of the ladder. "Can I come up?"

"No, baby. Okay, let's see, Doris's bed is about over here..." It was, as far as Mabs could tell, pretty near to the middle of the attic. With the plastic moved aside, she could see traces of sawdust on the floor, and squinted upward to see where it had come from.

The broken roof beam was almost directly above her. Jake nodded at a pale spot where she was standing. "Looks like there used to be a support beam there. And it wasn't..." He trailed off and took a utility knife out of his jeans pocket to slash apart the vapor barrier he'd wrapped around the broken roof beam. "It wasn't nailed or screwed in," he said when he'd pulled the plastic away to reveal the beam. "Just braced. You can see where it left an impression." He traced a space on the broken section of beam that matched the paler spot on the floor.

"So what happened?" Mabs asked, baffled. "Somebody removed it?"

"Looks like. There's no cut in the beam itself, but the wood's soft. You could tell that from the outside, though, with the break in the roof's spine. So I'd say it had mostly rotted a long time ago, and the support beam was all that was keeping it up. It was just waiting on a heavy snowfall, or even a bad storm, to come down."

"Bastards," Mabs said incredulously, even if she didn't know who the bastards were. "Why would somebody do th...to make me sell," she realized wearily. "Or to make Aunt Doris sell, before me. Shit, Jake. It has to be Preston, doesn't it? Only I don't know when, or how, or..."

"He came over to help with the house in September," Jake said in a low, angry voice.

"*Shit*. He *did*. And I know he was working inside the

house, but..." Mabs exhaled a sigh. "But I don't know how I'd prove anything. And he kept nagging and being nasty after that, but he stopped a few weeks ago, like he'd given up. There's no way he doesn't know the roof fell in. Everybody in Virtue knows. The judge had pictures on her phone, for heaven's sake. So why wouldn't he have started leaning on me again about it?" She looked for something to sit on, feeling defeated, but between shoveling snow out the window and moving everything that couldn't be shoveled, there was nothing left but cold bare floor.

"Well, your ex showed up around then, and you know everybody was talking about that, too. Maybe Preston figured if he shut up, you'd sell and leave with Brent."

"Ugh. I'm so glad the judge sent him packing. I still don't know how he even *found* us." Mabs went to lean on one of the small windows she'd shoveled snow through, staring down at the yard below. Brent had been out of her life so long, and she'd been cautious enough, that she really *didn't* know how he'd found her, but a shiver ran down her spine. "What if he didn't?"

Jake came to her side, frowning with curiosity. "Didn't what?"

"Find us." Mabs looked up at him. "What if someone found *him*?"

Jake's expression slowly cleared. "Somebody like Preston. But how could he? You didn't tell him Brent's name, did you?"

"No, but he knew Noah's, and..." Mabs bared her teeth. "And my mom's old-fashioned. She put a birth announcement about Noah in the paper, with Brent's name in it. I bet with my name, Noah's name, and a little effort, you could find it."

"You think Preston would go to that much trouble?"

Mabs lifted her eyebrows. "I dunno, you know him better than I do. But I think *Brent* wouldn't. He's never had to try for anything in his life. I can imagine it bugging him that he didn't know where I'd gone, but I can't imagine him bothering to do anything about it. I just don't know how I prove any of it."

"I could go have a chat with Brent," Jake offered with a kind of protective, not-quite-threatening growl to his voice. It sent a spill of delight through Mabs, and she stood on her toes to kiss him.

"That's nice of you, but it doesn't matter, I don't think. The judge got rid of him and I'm sure he didn't take the support beam out of the attic. If we could find a way to prove Preston did, though...."

"If I'd known to three months ago I could have sniffed around and found out, but any scent is long since gone."

Mabs grinned. "Sniff around. Literally. That's so cool. Okay, I'd better get back downstairs and make Noah—"

"Moooooooooommmmmmmmyyyyyyy? Wolf is *hungry*. Is it lunch time yet?"

"—some lunch," Mabs finished, and went to feed her poor perishing child and his dog.

CHAPTER 24

It bugged Jake that he couldn't pin anything on Preston Cole. In the grand scheme of things, Mabs was right: it didn't really matter. She'd kept the house, the roof could be repaired, and—

And she's our mate, his wolf said with satisfaction. *That's all we need.*

"It is," Jake said aloud, if softly. He'd gone to strip Doris's old bed while Mabs made lunch for Noah, and by the time he got everything into the washing machine, she'd finished and invited him to sit down and eat. Jake had, but absently, then went back up to the attic, hoping he could find something to tie Preston's presence that day to the broken roof beam.

Honestly, though, if the attic smelled of anything, it was old dust and cold air, neither of which was any use. He made himself busy lashing the roof beam back together, hating the hack job of it, but it was plywooded over, above that, and it wasn't likely another storm would break through the plywood. At the very least, they needed to finish clearing out that whole side of the house before he started doing real repair work, but it made him grumpy to think about it.

Late in the afternoon he and Mabs took Doris's bed apart and wrangled, with an enormous amount of effort, the bed's old mattress downstairs and onto the front porch. It weighed a ridiculous amount, even for a mattress, and just the idea of hauling it out to his truck so it could be brought to the dump left the adults panting with exhaustion. Noah and Wolf, delighted, spent half an hour jumping up and down on it, until Mabs finally said, "What if we put it on Noah's sled and dragged it over to the barn for him to play on until spring? We can throw it out then."

"The barn is farther away than my truck," Jake pointed out.

"True," she said. "But we don't have to *lift* it into the barn."

"Sold."

Mabs commandeered Noah's old-fashioned wood-slatted, metal-runnered sled, which he'd found in the barn himself, and they hauled the mattress out to the barn much more easily than it had come down the stairs. Noah and Wolf followed them and bounced merrily while Jake and Mabs flopped on the pallet bed Jake had been sleeping on until his move into the house. Mabs rubbed her hand over its surface, coming up with longish grey and white wolf hairs, and said, "You *were* sleeping as a wolf out here!"

"Silly not to use a built-in fur coat if you've got one." Jake pulled her close for a kiss, and then another, until they had to back away from each other, breathless, so that things wouldn't go too far while a four-year-old was ten feet away. "You are the most gorgeous woman I've ever met," he murmured. "I can't believe how lucky I am."

She laughed, a tiny, almost disbelieving sound. "*You're* lucky," she said, "*I'm* lucky. You're incredible. Skilled with your hands *and* devastatingly handsome."

"I am skilled with my hands, aren't I?" Jake pretended to pull her close again, making her laugh a second time.

"You are, but stop that." Mabs didn't sound like she *wanted* him to stop, but Noah, shrieking happily across the barn, would no doubt lose interest in bouncing on the old mattress if Jake tried to engage in any, uh, bouncing, of his own. Maybe trying to remind herself of that, Mabs rolled to the edge of the pallet bed and sat up, pushing her hands through her hair to get it away from her face. "Okay. I think that was everything in Doris's room. We can close it up now, until spring."

"Well..." Jake sat up, too. "I was thinking of going ahead and putting insulation strips into the floor and ceiling in there. It'll help."

Noah yelled, "Can I help?" and at Jake's agreement, bellowed, "Yaaay!" and fell onto his back on the mattress, clearly exhausted.

"Right. Okay. I'm going to finish moving things out of the parlor and downstairs bedroom, then. They got a lot of it in September, but if we're just winterizing that side of the house..." Mabs stood, stretching, then offered Jake a hand up. He took it, mostly for the excuse to curl her close when he stood, and she stole a kiss before they headed for the barn door.

"Mama, I'm gonna CAMP OUT in the barn FOREVER with Wolf, okay?"

"Okay, honey! See you at dinner time!"

Noah, evidently seeing no conflict between camping in the barn forever and coming in for dinner, shouted, "Okay!" at their backs.

Jake's wolf growled a warning as the barn door closed behind them, just before Jake himself caught a whiff of a familiar scent on the wind.

Brent Mitchell, and half a dozen near-strangers, stomped through Mabs's front gate.

MABS, under her breath, said, "What the hell?" and cast Jake a quick look that darted to the barn and back to him again. His gut clenched, but he nodded, slowing so he would remain between Noah and whatever trouble Mabs's ex had stirred up. He chafed a little, but his wolf preened with pride at being asked to protect the cub.

Wolves, Jake thought, were probably smarter than humans, at least in some ways.

Most.

A tense grin pulled at Jake's mouth as Mabs marched away from him. *Okay, maybe most.*

The little crowd Brent had gathered faltered as soon as they saw Mabs, glancing uncertainly at one another. Brent stalked forward, though, meeting her a bit closer to the barn than the house. "I'm taking my kid, Mabs, and nobody's gonna stop me. All these people," he waved at them, and it obviously stiffened their resolve a little, "have seen a wolf around here lately—"

"*Did* they?" Mabs sounded exactly like she did when Noah was telling her an incredibly unlikely story. "That's *amazing*. Where did they see it?" Jake was surprised she didn't add a 'honey' on the end of that, and fought off a grin.

"Right here," Brent snarled. "On this property. Hanging around this house."

Mabs made a show of leaning to one side, obviously taking a better look at the crew of men—mostly men, there was one woman—that Brent had rounded up. "Hey, Bill. Hi, Matt. Tonya. Gosh, I never even saw any of you at the house lately. Were you *spying* on me?" She said it like it was a game, not an accusation, and the guy who'd nodded when she'd said 'Matt' suddenly looked embarrassed.

"No, nah, nothing like that, Mabs. Just driving by, you know?"

"In your Toyota Leaf?" Mabs asked, encouragingly. "That cute little car? The one you can't see over the fence with? And you saw a wolf? Wow! Good job! How's that thing handling the snow, anyway? You must have to really watch the ruts in the road."

Jake's wolf, mystified, said, *what is she doing?* and Jake, biting the inside of his cheek to keep from laughing, said, *making them think about what they're doing.*

The wolf said, *oh,* and tipped its head dubiously. *Don't humans usually think about what they're doing?*

Far, far less than you'd imagine. Even as he talked with his wolf, Matt, obviously mortified, backed off, and another of the men with him did too, mumbling something about not really being able to see over the fence either.

"Well," Mabs said brightly, "you can get a glimpse through the gate sometimes, and goodness knows Noah's out here all the time with that puppy of his. I can see how things would get conf—"

"I didn't see a *puppy,*" Brent snarled. A couple of the others edged forward and Jake tensed, ready to cross the distance to Mabs's side and protect her. She was far enough away that a human wouldn't be able to hear their conversations so clearly, but he could, and would know if she really needed him.

"I know you've got a big truck, Tonya, you can probably see right over the fence. Gosh, can you tell me where the wolf was? If it was recently maybe I can check for tracks." Mabs was practically sparkling with innocent energy. Jake had to bite his lip to stop himself from grinning.

"No," Tonya said in a low voice. "It was back in the summer and I guess it was probably a big dog anyway, and probably up on Jen's property, now that I think about it."

"Oh, yeah, she's got the Rotties," Mabs said brightly. "I can see how you might think they were cows."

Jake choked on a laugh as Brent snapped, "Who said anything about *cows*?"

"I know, right? It was crazy!" Mabs spread her hands. "I was driving by Jen's ranch in July, I guess, and I looked out across the field and honestly for a second I thought they were cows too! Four of them, bouncing along like big sweet idiots, but they were so big and chonky I really did think they were cows!"

It was, Jake thought, like listening to Noah pick up pieces of what other people had said and put them together into an entirely new story that had nothing to do with anything at all. It was amazing, and the little group that Brent had dragged out were starting to look at each other like they not only doubted their own minds, but possibly Mabs's. And more importantly, Brent's, too.

"I figured it out after a second, of course," Mabs went on cheerfully, "but honestly, who would even think you could mistake dogs for cows?"

"What about *wolves*?!"

Mabs actually walked close enough to Brent to put a hand on his shoulder. Jake's whole body tensed, but she softened her voice and said, "Well, sure, Brent, people could mistake dogs for wolves, that would be easy. Look, I know you've had a rough time lately, so I think you should probably go tell Preston Cole that it didn't wo—"

"How did you know I was talking to Preston?!"

A huge amount of tension drained from Mabs's shoulders, visible even from the distance Jake was forcing himself to stay at. Her voice changed to sharp anger. "I didn't, Brent, but I sure as hell do now. Bill, Tonya, my ex doesn't give a damn about the safety of my son. I'm betting Preston Cole promised him a cut of the proceeds if he could get me off the Old Brannigan Place, and he's talked himself into believing there are wild animals around here that nobody's seen in fifty years.

"You all know me. Maybe not super well," she said with a nod to the people she hadn't named, "but we've seen each other around town. I want to be here, to be part of Virtue. I want my son to grow up here. All Brent and Preston want is for me to sell up so they can develop this whole stretch of land into a resort for rich people. Let's imagine for a minute there *were* wolves coming back to this area. That would be a conservation miracle. I'd hate to let somebody like *this*," and her tone conveyed the look of distaste she shot at Brent, "ruin what Virtue's spent such a long time building. I guess wolves must need some peace and tranquility, too, just like people."

"C'mon," said one of the strangers. "I don't know why I let this guy get me all worked up. Let's get out of here. I'll buy you a beer, Tonya, if you wanna meet at Hogan's. I'll buy everybody one, and we can have a little talk about Preston's development ideas."

"Yeah," Tonya said. "Sounds like a good idea to me." She broke from the group, and the others followed, leaving Brent standing on his own.

"It doesn't matter what they think, or how I found you," Brent growled. "I know what I saw and nobody's gonna convince me otherwise." Whatever else he had to say was drowned out by the sound of vehicles driving away.

In the silence afterward, with everyone else gone, Jake's wolf whispered, *Now??* and Jake, grinning, said, *Yeah. Now.*

He shifted, and with snarls and snapping teeth, chased Brent off the land for good.

"You should not have done that!" Mabs, laughing, threw herself into Jake's arms after he returned to his human form. "Oh my God, you shouldn't have done that! It was amazing, I've never heard anybody shriek like that, but what if he comes back? What if he—I don't know, what if he had a dashboard camera? What if he—"

Jake silenced her protestations with a kiss, and she didn't mind at all. "I had to," he informed her. "It was killing me, letting you be the fierce she-wolf and all, without me even getting a growl in. You were amazing." He spun her around and kissed her again. "You were *amazing*. You even got him to tell you Preston had looked him up!"

Joy bubbled through Mabs like golden sparkles, making her smile so widely it almost hurt. "I *was* amazing, wasn't I? I *did* get him to confess! But you! I thought you were gonna bite him!"

"I was not going to bite him," Jake assured her loftily. "For one thing, what if I'm wrong and it *did* turn him into a werewolf? That'd be the worst. But more importantly, biting him would leave evidence that there *was* a wolf around here."

"Oh, right. Good thinking. I still thought you were gonna bite him."

"He did too," Jake said smugly.

Mabs threw her arms around him again, hugging hard. "I'm so glad you're here. I'm so glad you're wonderful. I'm so glad you scared the pants off Brent. I hope we never see him again."

"I don't think we will. You were amazing," Jake said again, more softly. "A real she-wolf. I don't know how I could have ever doubted you were the woman for me." His gaze went distant a moment and he laughed. "My wolf wants you to know *he* never doubted it."

"Tell him he's very wise and handsome," Mabs said in the same placating tone she'd used on Brent's posse.

To her relief, Jake laughed. "He says you're right."

"Of course I am. Mommies are always right." Mabs gulped a breath and checked the time. "We only left Noah like ten minutes ago, right? That was relative time of being hours, not actual time? I was so freaked out."

"You came across as the least freaked-out person in history," Jake said. "And yeah, it was only a few minutes. Look, Mabs, I don't want to tell you what to do, but next time you need to face somebody down, can I do it? You're really good at it," he hastened to add, "but you've gotten to do it twice now and I want a chance." His gaze went distant again before he smiled crookedly. "My wolf says it's much more of an honor to protect the cubs and that humans don't understand what's important."

"Once more I agree with your wise and handsome wolf." Mabs stood on her toes to steal a kiss. "But yes, if there's a next time, I guess I can let you be the in-your-face hero. I don't really like it, but—"

"You're incredibly good at it."

She smiled. "Thanks. That wasn't what I was going to say, though. I was going to say, 'but Brent was my past coming back to haunt me, and I guess I felt like I had to face him.' Also, not to gang up on you by siding with your wolf, but..." She hesitated. "I can imagine somebody getting past me, Jake. I can't imagine someone getting past *you*, and that's what I want to have protecting my son."

"Yes," Jake almost howled, "but if you can't imagine somebody getting past me, and I'm protecting you *and* Noah, then you're both safe and nobody's gotten through you!"

Mabs pursed her lips, thinking her way through that, then had to shrug an agreement. "Okay, yeah, somehow I hadn't looked at it from that perspective. I'll let you be the big strong handsome front line from now on. Not that I plan to have any more showdowns."

"Maaaaammmmaaaa!" Noah's small voice, muffled by the barn, sounded distinctly guilty.

"Oh dear." Mabs pulled a face at Jake, muttered, "I

wonder what happened," and hurried back toward the barn, tugging Jake along behind her.

Noah appeared in the barn door before she got there, his little face concerned and his hands twisted behind his back. "I didn't *mean* to, Mama. It just *broke*."

"What broke, honey? Are you okay? Are you holding something?" Mabs let go of Jake's hand and crouched in front of her son, concern driving all other worries from her mind.

"I'm okay." Noah unfolded his hands from behind his back, displaying two fists full of cash. "But it *broke*."

Mabs actually heard herself wheeze like a cartoon character. Noah had fifties crushed in his hands, a lot of them, and, as she looked over his shoulder into the barn, she could see a trail of them behind him, scattered across the barn floor. "Noah, where, uh, where did you get these..."

"The mattress broke," he said miserably. "The dollars fell out."

Jake, standing behind Mabs, said, "Oh my God," in a fascinated tone, and pushed the doors open so they could follow the bills back to the mattress.

A velcroed seam had split open from Noah's bouncing, and more fifties, as well as tens and twenties, were smooshed through it. Mabs dropped to her knees, echoing Jake's, "Oh my God," in a squeak.

Noah, miserable with worry, wailed, "I didn't *mean* to!" and Mabs fumbled him into a hug.

"It's okay, baby. You're fine. It was an accident, and besides, this mattress is made to break like that. Maybe not from being bounced on, but..." Her ability to talk, or even think, simply faded, and she just stared at the split in the mattress seam.

Jake knelt beside her and pulled the seam open farther. More bills spilled out, like they'd been dying to escape. Mabs and Jake both croaked a laugh, and Jake picked up a few of the bills before letting his hand fall. "No wonder the mattress weighed so much. Oh my God. We nearly threw it away."

"Who keeps money in a *mattress* ?" Mabs's voice shot high, then disappeared again into a nervous laugh.

"Sarah did," Jake said in a voice an awful lot like the one she'd just used. "I mean, Sarah said all the rich Virtue-ese kept their wealth in their mattresses, but I didn't think she *meant* it!"

"I'm sure she didn't, but...!" Mabs gestured helplessly at the mattress. She was afraid to even open it any more, like the cash would disappear like leprechaun gold.

Noah, who had stuffed a hand in his mouth, extracted it to say, "Are we rich now, Mommy?"

Mabs laughed again, still high and nervous-sounding. "Not after we're done paying off the house repairs, no, honey, but we're not in the hole, either."

Noah looked around with interest. "What hole?"

"No, not like an actual hole, honey, it just means, uh, owing people money. Oh my God. Am I really seeing this?"

Jake had pulled the seam open even farther as she spoke, and money really did just slide out onto the barn floor. "She must have been avoiding banks for decades. My God, look at all this. This is..."

"This isn't a money." Noah shoved his hand into the growing pile of cash and extracted a piece of brightly colored cloth.

"How did you even see that," Mabs breathed, taking it from him. It was square, neatly hemmed, and crumpled from having been compressed in wads of cash for heaven knew how long. It also looked vaguely familiar, and Mabs stared at it a few seconds before shrieking and dropping it as she jerked backward. "Oh my God. Oh my God. That's one of Preston's handkerchiefs!"

"What the hell is it doing in—" Jake's breath caught sharply and he cut himself off as Noah blinked between the adults with wide-eyed interest. He cleared his throat and rose. "I'll, um. I'll go call..."

Mabs nodded and carefully put the handkerchief back down in the money. "Yeah. You, uh. You go do that." Jake left the barn while Noah tried to grab the hankie again, and instead Mabs caught his hands and then picked him up, upside-down. "We have to leave this stuff here for a while, baby. We'll get to figure out what to do with it later. In the meantime, would you like some lun...dinner?"

"Lundinner!" Noah howled at her hip, gleefully. "What's lundinner?"

"It's leftover peanut butter and jelly sandwiches fried like fish sticks."

"YUMMY! I want that!"

"Well, I walked into that," Mabs muttered, then brightened her voice as she carried Noah out of the barn, Wolf bouncing around her feet. "Did you leave any PBJ sandwiches left over?"

"Noooooooooo..."

"I guess we'll just have to have fish sticks, then."

"Can we have..." Noah, dangling, fell silent as he tried to think of something spectacular enough to justify the ask. Jake, up ahead of them, nearly at the house, turned back to lift his chin in a kind of reverse nod that suggested he'd called the police, and that they were on the way. "Pizza?" Noah finally asked, with the kind of desperate enthusiasm that suggested he simply hadn't been able to come up with a better proposal.

"How about spaghetti and meatballs?"

"Yesssssssssss!" Noah squirmed until Mabs had to put him down for fear of dropping him. Then, Wolf at his heels, he ran off to play while Mabs went to sag against the side of the house with Jake.

"I have to heat up dinner," she said quietly, "but...um. Wow."

"The sheriff is on his way," Jake said with a nod. "He'll probably want to talk to you more than me. I'll wrangle Noah, if necessary."

Joy and relief flooded her and she stepped into his arms, hugging him. "Thank you."

"What are partners for?"

A spasm of nervous delight shot through her. "Is that what we are now? Partners?"

Jake wrinkled his face. "I know it's diving right in, but I thought we could just skip the girl-friend/boyfriend thing, maybe?"

"Yeah." Mabs kissed him, then hugged him hard again, glad to be with him. "Yeah, that sounds great to me. Okay. I'm going to throw dinner together before the sheriff gets here, and...wow. This is going to be a lot."

"We'll get through it," Jake promised. "Together."

THE SHERIFF CAME and went in far less time than Mabs expected, but four hours later her phone rang with Sarah's picture coming up. Noah was in bed already, so Mabs put it on speaker and lay the phone down on the coffee table between herself and Jake so they could both hear Sarah say, "What the hell *happened*, Mabs, the city council chat group is *buzzing* about Preston Cole's arrest!"

Mabs said, "Oh my God," softly, and moved closer to Jake, but Sarah went on as if she hadn't spoken.

"Everybody's saying he just up and confessed to murdering Doris Brannigan, but that can't be right. He'd never just say it. What happened? Did you find some dirt on him? Tell me everything!"

"We found one of his handkerchiefs in—" Mabs broke off, glanced at Jake, and, evasively, said, "In her bedroom. And her diary talked about him harassing her. I don't know what happened, exactly, but the sheriff must have gotten him to confess. Holy crap," she added for good measure, and Sarah's laugh burst over the line.

"Holy crap indeed! Preston! Who would have thought he had it in h—actually I guess I kinda did," she said with less humor. "I mean, he really was always a jerk."

"He's the one who told my ex where to find me, too," Mabs said with a sigh. "But that's over, too, Judge Owens ruled in my favor and Jake, uh, scared him off this afternoon."

"By being a wolf," Sarah said solemnly as Mabs and Jake both choked and stared at each other. "I heard," Sarah went on. "Excellent party trick. Look, I really just wanted to call to see if you two were okay. Are you okay?"

"Yeah," Mabs said softly. "I didn't know about the arrest, but...yeah. We're okay. Thanks for checking on us."

She hung up and turned to Jake, who said, "Holy crap."

Mabs really thought that summed it up. "Jake, what do we do with a mattress full of money?"

"Honestly, I'd probably put it in a different mattress and start paying off bills," Jake admitted. "Of course, the sheriff knows about it and might have a different opinion on more formal things to do with it, but I don't think there's any doubt it's your money, Mabs. And I don't think it's *enough* money to fall under the estate taxes stuff, although I guess we could count it to find out."

"We should probably count it, at least, just so we know how much is there."

"I want to get some rubber gloves first," he said, making a face. "It's called 'filthy lucre' for a reason, and somebody's been sleeping on that for decades. I hate to think how many skin cells are in there."

"Well, that's about the most disgusting thing I've ever heard."

"You," Jake said, "are the mother of a small child. I *absolutely* do not believe that's the grossest thing you've ever heard, or done, or touched."

Mabs made a face, then made another one. "Touché. I won't regale you with the details. Okay. Rubber gloves and cash-counting tomorrow, I guess, and...and then, I don't know, do you think we could just take things nice and quiet and easy until, like, Christmas?"

"Oh, I don't know," Jake murmured. "Christmas is what, three weeks away? I can think of a *lot* of things to do that are nice, but not quiet, and might be easy, for three weeks..." He leaned in to kiss her, and then again, until they really weren't on the couch anymore, and both of them were in danger of getting rug burns from too much vigorous activity on the floor.

ASIDE FROM NOCTURNAL activities with Jake, paying off bills over the next few weeks was honestly one of the best feelings Mabs had ever experienced. All *sorts* of rumors flew around Virtue about where the money had come from, with Mabs's favorite being "Old Ms. Brannigan left a mattress full of money for them to find," because nobody actually believed it. She just said, "My ship finally came in," when people asked, and they went on imagining mattresses and buried treasures and attic antiques sold for a small fortune.

Christmas rolled around with less stress than Mabs

had ever experienced, in part because she had no outstanding bills, but mostly because Jake was happy to stay up late wrapping gifts with her, and because Noah was overwhelmed with excitement at the upcoming holiday. To her confusion, Jake kept her out of the kitchen all day, but she couldn't exactly complain about the promise of a Christmas feast she didn't have to cook herself.

Finally, after much thumping and crashing and a lot of astonishingly good smells, around four p.m. she was invited into the kitchen for the first time all day. The table was set, but a space had been left for an enormous gift box that had Noah's name on an equally enormous tag. He yelled with delight and pulled it apart, then gave a gasp that even Mabs found gratifying, despite being not at all responsible for the gift within.

Noah, with more care than Mabs had ever seen him use, took out first one, then another, then another and another, hand-built wooden train cars, and then dozens upon dozens of pieces of track that all fit together. The train was brightly painted, its grooved wheels fitting onto the tracks perfectly. Noah took them all out, then sat there, his eyes wide and his mouth wider, trying to take it all in before he finally whispered, "Did you make all this, Mr. Growly?"

"I did," Jake said gently. Mabs pressed her fingers over her mouth, trying not to cry as he asked, "Do you like it?"

"It's *almost* as good as *Wolf*," Noah whispered, and threw himself at Jake's legs to hug them. "Thank you, Mr. Growly!"

"Ah, you're welcome, Noah." Jake picked the little boy up and hugged him. Mabs gave up trying not to cry and wiped at her eyes as Jake pulled her into the hug too, then murmured, "Do you see your gift?"

"Mine? You mean besides dinner? No, what..." Wiping her eyes again, she turned, looking around the kitchen.

Something seemed... *off*. Mabs frowned, looking around again, then moved away from the other two, trying to put her finger on it.

And then she *did* put her finger on it, literally, as she reached for a cabinet door and realized that she could reach not just its bottom shelf, but its upper one as well. She jolted, then spun around, staring at the cupboards.

They had *all* been lowered to a height she could reach. Every single one of the upper shelves had been moved down at least six inches, revealing paler wood above them where they'd once hung. "Oh my God! Jake! Jake! You moved the cabinets so I could reach them! That's the nicest thing anybody has ever done for me!"

She turned toward him, her jaw gaping just like Noah's had been, and found Jake Rowly on one knee on her kitchen floor, an open black velvet box in one hand and a sparkling-eyed little boy crawling up his back with a train engine in one hand. "Um," Jake said, rolling his head back a little toward Noah, "this part, um, this part isn't exactly what I planned, but—"

Mabs put her hands over her mouth, tears rolling down her cheeks. "But it's perfect," she whispered.

"But it's perfect," Jake agreed in little more than a

whisper himself. "Mary Anne Brannigan, will you please marry me?"

"Yes! Yes! Yes, I will!" Mabs fell to her knees and Jake caught her in a hug and Noah smashed her head with his train engine, and it was, in fact, *perfect*.

~THE END~

ABOUT THE AUTHOR

Some say Murphy Lawless is the descendant of Irish gangsters, exiled to Australia, who has made good on the family name. It's probably true*.

But then, others claim that Murphy was a spy for the Allies during the war. Stories are told of daring rescues of intrepid reporters from almost certain death, but Murphy has never admitted to anything. Still others say Lawless studied with a local tribe for years after crash-landing in the untamed wilds, having accepted a dare from a pilot of ill repute, and came away from the experience a kinder, wiser, gentler soul.

Even now, though, the most widely held belief is that Lawless left Australia as a mere slip of a thing, and made a fortune in the wilds of the Alaskan oil fields before realizing that romance was the ultimate adventure. Murphy now writes passionate, fun-filled stories of paranormal romance and destined love.

*Probably.

You can find Murphy at CatieMurphy.com, Patreon, and at her newsletter, which is by far the best way to have up-to-date information delivered straight to you!

www.ingramcontent.com/pod-product-compliance
Lightning Source LLC
Chambersburg PA
CBHW030925210726
48290CB00007B/2077